D0330930

double eagle

double
eagle

SNEED B. COLLARD III

Ω
PEACHTREE
ATLANTA

PEACHTREE PUBLISHERS
1700 Chattahoochee Avenue
Atlanta, Georgia 30318-2112

www.peachtree-online.com

Cover design by Maureen Withee
Book composition by Melanie McMahon Ives

Printed January 2011 in the United States of America by Lake Book Manufacturing in
Melrose Park, Illinois

10 9 8 7 6 5 4 3

Library of Congress Cataloging-in-Publication Data

Collard, Sneed B.
  Double eagle / written by Sneed B. Collard III. -- 1st ed.
    p. cm.
  Summary: In 1973, Michael and Kyle's discovery of a rare Confederate coin at an old
Civil War fort turns into a race against time as the boys try to find more coins before a
hurricane hits Alabama's Gulf coast.
  Includes bibliographical references (p.).
  ISBN 978-1-56145-480-8 / 1-56145-480-X
  [1. Coins--Collectors and collecting--Fiction. 2. Buried treasure--Fiction. 3. Hurri-
canes--Fiction. 4. Alabama--History--1951---Fiction.] I. Title.
  PZ7.C67749Dq 2009
  [Fic]--dc22
                                    2008036746

For my father

—*S. B. C. III*

APRIL 24, 1862

The Alabama coast—April 24, 1862

*E*ven in the darkness of the pilothouse, the knuckles of the captain's hands gleamed bone white. He gripped the wheel of the Skink and peered out at the dim silhouette of Fort Morgan, one of two forts guarding the mouth of Mobile Bay. Both forts were in Confederate hands, and while the captain kept his boat within the protective reach of their cannon, he knew he was safe. But now, following the directions of his pilot, the captain steered the Skink past the forts and out into the Gulf of Mexico—Federal gunboat territory. With each chuff of the paddle wheel steamer's engines, he could feel the blood thicken inside his veins.

It had been a harrowing week for the captain, and indeed for all sons and daughters of the Confederacy. For months, rumors of a Union attack on New Orleans had swirled all along the Gulf Coast. Finally, a few days earlier, Confederate spies had confirmed the news: an attack was imminent. Throughout the Crescent City civilians and soldiers scrambled to defend and, in many cases, flee the

South's most important port. Several local businessmen had hired the Skink to whisk both personal and commercial freight to the safety of Havana, Cuba. But as the steamer was preparing to leave, a Confederate major had unexpectedly arrived with an additional cargo chest. The major ordered the chest taken not to Havana, but to Fort Henry at the mouth of Mobile Bay.

"But that's well out of our way!" the captain had protested. "It will put us in added danger from Union warships!"

The major showed little sympathy. "Agree now or I will commandeer this vessel for military duty."

The captain's mouth opened, then closed again. His choice was made. And in case the captain had any second thoughts, the major left two soldiers on the vessel to make sure his orders were executed.

As the Union Fleet assembled to begin shelling the defenses that protected New Orleans, the Skink slipped out into the Gulf of Mexico under cover of darkness. That night the captain cursed his fortune. If it weren't for the last-minute command to deliver the mysterious chest, he would already be running through open water toward Havana. Instead he was forced to hug the coastline, on constant alert for fickle currents, shifting sandbars, and Union gunboats.

But throughout the rest of the night and the next day, his luck held. The Union blockade was still in its infancy and posed only a modest threat to Confederate shipping. Besides, the captain reasoned, the Union navy undoubtedly had its hands full with the attack on New Orleans. As they passed from New Orleans to Pascagoula, Mississippi, the captain didn't spot a single Union vessel. Even better, a new moon and thick cloud cover helped obscure the Skink from enemy eyes. Twenty-four hours after leaving New Orleans, just after sunset, the Skink steamed safely through the western access channel to Mobile Bay and docked at the pier of Fort Henry.

Following the major's instructions, the captain handed over the mystery chest to the fort's commander. Brigadier General Josiah Buckford seemed surprised by the delivery.

"What are its contents?" he asked the captain.

The captain looked at the two soldiers who had accompanied him. They shrugged and one responded, "Ain't no one told us, sir."

"I also do not know," the captain told General Buckford.

"Very well." Turning to several soldiers on the pier, the general barked, "Take the chest to my quarters. Do not open it." Then, returning his attention to the captain, he said, "Allow us to offer you refreshment after your journey. I would like to hear your observations on the situation in N'Orleans."

"Thank you, sir," the captain replied, looking up at the cloud-covered night sky, "but if it's all the same to you, I'd like to get underway while we still have concealment of darkness and the tide runs high."

The general nodded. "I understand."

After taking on more coal, the Skink chugged away from the dock. Instead of heading out of Mobile Bay's main entrance, the captain chose the preferred route of blockade-runners and made his way to the easternmost channel, the one protected by the guns of Fort Morgan. The fort slipped by to the port side without incident, and after running along the coast for another mile the captain spun the wheel starboard, turning the Skink south toward open waters. Two miles from shore the captain began to breathe more deeply. Finally they were safe.

Then, without warning, the pilot shouted, "Captain! A Union warship!"

"Full steam!" the captain ordered, but even as the words left his mouth, he saw the warship's outline less than half a mile away. He knew that their situation was dire.

"Perhaps they do not see us," the pilot said.

A warning shot from the Union vessel erased any doubts.

"Raise sails!" the captain ordered his crew. "We need every breath of speed we can muster."

"Shouldn't we surrender?" the pilot asked. "We don't stand a chance against their cannon."

"Silence! I will not spend the rest of the war rotting in a Yankee prison or turn over my boat to the Union cause!"

But the warship was already bearing down. Another warning shot rent the night air.

"More steam, man!" the captain shouted at his engineer.

"The boilers will overheat!"

Just then the captain looked out to see the warship turning to a full broadside position. His throat filled with bile and before he could give another order, the Union gunboat's deadly cannon opened fire.

JUNE 1973

Chapter 1

The Divorce Shuffle stinks. I knew from firsthand experience: It was my fourth summer flying across the country from California to Florida to visit my dad. It wasn't that I didn't want to see him. In fact, the opposite was true. I missed my father all year long and couldn't wait to be with him again. But the transition, well, that was tough.

Life with my mom and stepdad in California followed a comfortable routine. On school days we got up at six-thirty, ate toast and eggs for breakfast, and left the house by eight. After school, if it was cross-country or track season, I stayed for practice. If not, I caught the bus home, changed my clothes, and took off riding bikes with the other guys in the neighborhood. Dinner at six o'clock sharp. Homework. Then my favorite time of the day. I dug out my coin collection and spread it out on my desk. I powered up my new Pioneer SX-454 receiver, put on the headphones, and dialed in the latest tracks from Led Zeppelin, the Rolling Stones, and the Who on the world's greatest radio station, KMET-FM in Los Angeles. After an hour or two rocking out and poring over my latest coin finds, I flopped into bed to rest up for another, almost identical day.

Okay, so it wasn't the most thrilling existence, but it was comfortable. I knew what to expect.

Not so with my dad.

Unlike my mom, my dad hadn't remarried. He'd had girlfriends now and then, but nothing had stuck. No surprise. My dad…well, he did what he wanted to—a habit that didn't exactly nurture long-term relationships. After finishing his PhD at the University of California at Santa Barbara, he'd landed a job as a biology professor at the University of West Florida in Pensacola. During my six to eight weeks with him each summer, the days were as unpredictable as the Gulf Coast's turbulent weather.

Some days my dad would shake me awake and announce an expedition to look for turtles or snakes or pitcher plants. Other days he'd take me out to his lab and put me to work inhaling formaldehyde fumes while I sorted samples of sargassum weed he'd collected in the Gulf of Mexico. Many days, while he worked on a grant proposal or scientific paper, I'd read adventure novels or look for alligators down at the campus bayou. To my friends back home, this all sounded groovy, and I have to admit that except for the formaldehyde, I liked it pretty well.

But it was also a big adjustment. That first week my dad always managed to tick me off somehow—by accident or on purpose, I could never be sure. Only after we got into a big fight or two did things settle down enough for me to embrace the new routine, or lack of it.

This year, though, my dad decided to throw something entirely new at me—something that caused me more than my usual level of "arrival anxiety." As soon as he picked me up at the Pensacola Airport, he whisked me across the Alabama state line in his beige VW Squareback. He drove us under the city of Mobile through the Bankhead Tunnel. Then, we rattled down the west side of Mobile Bay toward a place called Shipwreck Island, where he had taken a summer job teaching invertebrate zoology at a brand-new marine lab. It was there, not Pensacola, where I would be spending the next two months.

As our beige beast bumped onto the three-mile-long drawbridge that reached out from the mainland, I saw the long silhouette of Shipwreck Island looming dark and mysterious across the sun-splattered surface of the Intracoastal Waterway. My stomach knotted and I began counting my teeth with the tip of my tongue, something I always did when I was nervous. *What will our living quarters there be like?* I worried. *How many new people will I have to meet? What am I going to do all summer while Dad is teaching? Why can't he just stay in one place like a normal parent?*

I would soon learn the answers—at least to my first three questions.

* * *

After crossing the drawbridge we passed through a little village, if you could call it that. A large marina with about a hundred boats filled the protected inlet to our left. On the right sat a gas station, a restaurant, a couple of houses, and a store called "Bait 'n Stuff." The Bait 'n Stuff looked like the main game on the island for shopping of any kind, and it featured a hand-painted sign that read "Best Tamales This Side 'a Pascagoula."

I laughed, momentarily forgetting my anxiety.

"Did I miss something?" my dad asked.

I pointed to the sign. "Are there *any* other tamales this side of Pascagoula?"

My dad grinned. "I see your point."

At a T intersection we turned left and rumbled down a long, straight road through a forest of pine, oak, and palmetto. Here and there another road opened up on either side, and I glimpsed a few houses tucked among the trees. Two miles later, we reached a treeless expanse that seemed to encompass the entire eastern tip of the island.

A sign read "South Coast University Marine Laboratories." My dad slowed and turned right through an open chain-link gate. I squinted at a collection of bleached cinder-block buildings that looked more like a prison than a place of higher learning. We parked in front of a long, two-story, whitewashed building that sat squat and permanent, as though it had been carved from a single, massive block of concrete.

"Welcome to SCUM-Lab," my father said, using the nickname the place had acquired during its first year of operation. "Whaddya think?"

"It's not the Holiday Inn," I observed.

My dad chuckled. "You're right. At Holiday Inns, the roaches don't eat nearly as well. Let's go check out our accommodations."

My dad had already told me that until recently the lab had been a United States Air Force radar base. The base had been constructed to withstand a nuclear attack, which explained the bleak, durable construction of the dormitory and other buildings. When the base closed, Alabama's major universities had petitioned Congress to turn it over to the university system for a marine biology lab. It was obvious that they'd forgotten to ask for any money to fix the place up.

I trailed my dad up the front staircase to the second-floor hallway of the monolithic whitewashed building.

"This was the base barracks for enlisted men," my dad said. "Now it's Home Sweet Home."

He stopped outside of Room 208, inserted a key, and opened the door. I entered to find a cell-block room inhabited by a sagging double bed, a dresser with peeling veneer, and a desk with enough coffee cup rings on it to make a dozen Olympic flags.

I studied the bed. "We're sharing that?" I asked, already

dreading the prospect of sleeping next to my dad's chain-saw snore.

"It's not quite as grim as it looks," he said. "We're lucky. We got a deluxe suite."

I followed him into the walk-through bathroom and out the other side to a second bedroom. "See?" he said. "You get a room all to yourself."

The relief must have showed on my face. My dad laughed and punched me on the shoulder. "Don't look so glum. You're going to like it here," he told me.

How would you know? I wanted to say, but I kept my mouth shut.

"Come on," he said. "I'll give you the grand tour."

* * *

Leaving our "deluxe suite," we clattered down the rear metal fire escape of the barracks. Even before we reached the bottom I heard the lightning crack of billiard balls smashing together.

"Sounds like someone's in the rec room," my dad said.

We walked through an open door to find three men clustered around a pool table. One guy was leaning forward over the table, cue poised for a shot, but he straightened up when he saw us. "Hey, Doc!"

"Hey, Doc yourself," my dad said. "Professor Robert Halsted, this is my son Michael."

"Call me Bob," the man told me. Professor Halsted looked about my dad's age—in his midthirties or so—and was also my dad's height of about five foot ten. His medium-length brown hair hung down his neck and a scruffy, untrimmed beard wrapped around his chin. "Welcome to Alabama," he said, his handshake warm and friendly.

My dad turned to the second man. "Rod, my son Michael." At six foot three or so, Rod towered over everyone else in the room. Younger than Professor Halsted—in his early twenties, I guessed—Rod had a deeply tanned face and a full head of curly hair that poofed out like a sun-bleached sea sponge. He wore a string of beads around his neck, but I guessed they were there to look cool, not to promote peace, love, and understanding.

"Rod's in my invert class," my dad explained.

I expected Rod to shake hands with me too, or at least show some interest. Instead he just mumbled, "Hey, kid" and returned his attention to the pool table.

Finally my dad turned to the last person in the room. "And Mike, this is the boy I've been telling you about, Kyle Daniels."

My dad used the word "boy," but Kyle Daniels looked well on his way to becoming a man. He stood only an inch or so taller than I did, but in that yellow tank top his shoulders looked half again as wide as mine. His almost-white hair hung straight and shaggy over his sunburned ears, and his blue eyes glinted even before he said anything.

Kyle stepped forward and stuck out his hand. "How ya doin', Michael?" He flashed me a smile so bright my pupils groaned.

"I'm okay," I muttered.

"I've been telling Kyle you were coming," my dad said.

Kyle nodded. "Yeah. Glad to have you around. This place can get a little dead."

"Mmm-hmm." You'd think I'd also be glad to have Kyle around, especially marooned out on an island at the very tip of Alabama.

I wasn't.

Kyle's presence was just one more uncertainty I had to deal with. One more relationship I had to work out. Worse, I realized, he represented something I usually didn't have to deal with in the summers—*competition*. My dad had already told me that Kyle was a year older than me— fifteen to my fourteen. What my father hadn't mentioned was that Kyle was also stronger and better-looking than me. And his annoyingly cheery smile probably meant that he had a great personality. If that wasn't enough, Kyle had gotten here before me and had a chance to get in good with everyone before I arrived. Didn't my dad's student Rod blow me off just the moment before?

No, I wasn't happy about Kyle Daniels. Sixty seconds after meeting him, I wished a tornado would roar down on Shipwreck Island and blow him away.

Chapter 2

After leaving the rec room my dad and I walked back out to our VW. He lugged my suitcase up to our quarters and I followed behind, carrying my running bag and the blue canvas AWOL bag that held a couple of my coin albums. My entire collection was way too big to drag here from California, but I'd brought my Jefferson nickel and Lincoln cent books to pick away at during the summer, along with the latest edition of the *Red Book* pricing guide.

As I dumped my bags onto my bed, my father said, "Well, Jed, welcome back to the Deep South."

I smiled at our old inside joke and answered, "Why thank ya, Pa. It ain't much, but it's home."

"You hungry, Jed? It's about chow time."

"I reckon I could eat."

"The mess hall's open. Let's mosey on over."

From our barracks we walked across the oyster shell parking lot to the one-story dining hall. My dad introduced me to several other faculty members and students as we inched our way forward in the cafeteria-style serving line. I kept an eye out for Kyle Daniels, hoping we wouldn't have to sit with him, and my luck held. I spotted him sitting at a full table with people I assumed to be his parents and younger sister. After collecting heaping plates of fried mullet, corn bread, and collard greens, my dad and I sat down several tables away, across from Professor Halsted. Next to him sat a young woman with dark hair pulled back into a floppy ponytail. She wore a black tank top that revealed some serious cleavage. The way her eyes darted flirtatiously around the room, I assumed she was one of the students.

"Michael—or do you go by Mike?" Professor Halsted asked as we sat down.

"Mike's fine."

"Well, Mike, I want you to meet my wife Becky."

I stopped chewing. This sex goddess was Professor Halsted's wife?

Becky's eyes slid toward me. "Nice to meetcha, Michael," she purred.

I choked out a barely audible "hi" and reached for my iced tea.

Becky wasn't the only pleasant surprise in the room. A steady stream of tanned, trim college girls or women—I couldn't figure out what to call them—paraded into the mess hall. Some wore tank tops or loose T-shirts. Others wore nothing but short shorts and bikini tops.

Hmmm, I thought. *SCUM-Lab is looking better and better.*

Then I reminded myself that I'd never even kissed a girl—any girl—much less a woman who looked like this. *Yeah,* I sighed, coming back to earth. It promised to be yet another frustrating summer on the girl front.

"You play volleyball?"

"Huh?" I swung my attention back to Professor Halsted. "Yeah. A little."

"I never met a Californian who didn't," he said with a wink. "We've got a pickup game after dinner. You in?"

"I guess so."

* * *

One good thing about living on an old Air Force base, I discovered, was that the military had installed recreational facilities to keep its men from shooting each other or declaring war on Mississippi out of boredom. One of these facilities was an outdoor swimming pool near the beach, and next to the pool someone had staked out a sand volleyball court with a sagging net.

Teams formed up and I found myself playing with my dad, Professor Halsted, and a couple of students. To my relief, Kyle wasn't on our team. He was playing on the other side with Professor Halsted's wife Becky and Rod—the tall, stuck-up student of my dad's I'd met in the rec room earlier.

Once the game started I quickly realized that most of them played "jungle ball," smacking the ball around haphazardly or trying to show off with sloppy, heroic spikes.

My junior high in California had a volleyball team, but I'd never gone out for it, opting for cross-country and track instead. I'd played volleyball in PE, though, and I was pretty good at it—at least compared to the people around me now.

As the ball sallied back and forth over the net, I dug some hard, low balls off the sand and passed the ball easily to the people on the front row.

"Hey, Jed," my dad called when I blocked a shot on the net. "Nice play!"

"You didn't tell us you had a ringer over there," a great-looking brunette named Linda called from the opposite team.

I got ready for the next serve, praying that I wasn't blushing.

But even while I was distracted by the game—and the bikini tops around me—I couldn't help making a couple of observations. One was that my dad's student Rod and Professor Halsted's wife Becky seemed awfully chummy. They joked and flirted with each other like a couple of ghost crabs doing a mating dance. Once when a ball came near them they crashed into each other and Rod accidentally wrapped his long claws—I mean arms—around her waist. They both laughed loudly, and I glanced over at Professor Halsted, expecting him to race over and clobber Rod, but he just smiled along with the good times. I didn't know what to make of that.

The second thing I noticed was that Kyle was getting

frustrated trying to pass and hit the ball. He obviously didn't have any training at the game, and he fumbled and carried it badly.

Maybe, I said to myself, *this is my chance to put Kyle Daniels in his place and stake out my territory.*

After every service change our team rotated. Through the first game Kyle and I were positioned too far apart to interact, but near the end of the second game, I found myself in the front center position, opposite Kyle.

"You play good," he told me.

"Thanks," I muttered, looking back as a student on our side prepared for his serve.

The ball soared over the net and the other team batted it around a couple of times, then sent it flying back to our side. My dad hit it over to Professor Halsted and it again crossed the net. Rod hit a moon ball to Kyle, who jumped to spike it. I was ready. I leaped high, and Kyle hit the ball right into my splayed hands, deflecting it back onto his side. Our point.

"Way to go, Mike!" a guy on our team called.

Kyle forced a grin and said, "Good one."

Our team served again. Kyle's team fielded it and knocked it to the back row of our side. A girl in a green bikini swung wildly and got lucky. The ball shot straight up, hung in the air for a split second, and came down in my direction in the front row. The ball was a little too close to the net and I knew I should just tap it over, but I got greedy. As the ball tumbled toward us Kyle and I leaped into the air at the same time. I could already visualize spiking the ball right into Kyle's face and earning myself yet more glory.

I judged the ball's trajectory and swung with all my might. Big mistake. I hit the ball with the heel of my hand and it rocketed straight over, sailing twenty feet out of bounds. Worse, I caught my arm in the net and landed entangled like a gilled mullet in the surf zone.

"Nice try," Professor Halsted said.

"Yeah, Jed," my dad said.

I felt my face turn as pink as a conch shell.

So much for showing up Kyle Daniels.

Chapter 3

The next morning I awakened to the sounds of a construction crew pounding an arsenal of hammers. At least that's what I thought was going on until I pulled myself out of la-la land and realized someone was knocking on my door.

"What the—?" I muttered, struggling out of bed.

I tugged on my cutoffs and stumbled like a zombie for the doorknob.

"Hey, Mike!" Kyle's grinning face looked altogether too exuberant for so early in the morning.

"What time is it?"

"'Bout nine. You missed breakfast, but Louella'll find you somethin' if you hurry on over."

"Oh."

"Anyhow, I was about to take my sister fishin' over at one of the jetties by the fort. Thought you might want to come along."

"Fishing?"

"I got an extra pole, you need it."

I liked to fish, even though the world's fish population had signed an international agreement to stay away from my bait. What I didn't feel like doing was hanging around this Southern hick and his sister.

"Uh, thanks, but I'm not feeling all that great this morning," I lied.

Kyle took it in stride. "Oh, hey. I know what that's like. Maybe later."

"Yeah. Maybe."

Closing the door, I felt a twinge of guilt but couldn't pinpoint why. I didn't owe this guy anything.

I splashed water on my face, put on my sandals and a T-shirt, and crunched over the oyster shells to the mess hall, my stomach rumbling. Just as Kyle had promised, Louella saved me. She was a large woman—picture a manatee wearing a white blouse and lime green pants—but her smile shone like a piano keyboard under a spotlight.

"Why, hello there, hon," she said as soon as I stumbled in. Her kind eyes gave me a quick once-over. "You must be seriously jet-laggin'."

"Yeah," I admitted. "A little."

"You poor thing. Well, me an' Evelyn'll be glad to fix you right up."

Evelyn—she pronounced it Ev-o-line—waved at me from the stove and set to work scrambling some eggs, which Louella then heaped over hash browns and grits.

"Thanks," I said, trying to keep from drooling.

"You don' mention it, hon. We're jes' glad to have y'all

with us. Your daddy's done nothin' but talk about you since he got here."

I wondered if that were true, but I was too hungry to give it much thought. I chose an empty table—an easy task since I was the only person in the room—and pounced on my meal like a starving raccoon. I'd about cleaned my plate when a golden-skinned goddess walked into the mess hall. She wore short white shorts and a bronze bikini top that matched the color of her flawless tan. I recognized her as Linda, the student who'd paid me a compliment at the volleyball game the night before.

"There you are!" she exclaimed.

I glanced over my shoulder. She couldn't possibly be talking to me.

"Yes, you," she said, striding toward me on the most perfect set of legs I'd ever laid eyes on.

"Oh, hi." As I spoke, a small hunk of grits flew out of my mouth and stuck to the hairs of my right arm. Linda pretended not to notice.

"Hey, listen," she said, pouring her words like warm syrup. "I just talked to your dad. I'm Linda, by the way. Linda Garcon—with a *c,* not an *s.*"

She stuck out her hand and I shook it, my palm sweaty.

"I'm in your dad's invert class, and he said you could go out collecting with me this morning. Interested?"

Does a dog wag his tail? I wanted to say, but instead I blurted, "Sure!" Suddenly I felt extremely happy I hadn't gone fishing with Kyle Daniels and his sister.

"Great," Linda said. "Meet me over at the dock. It's

right across the road from the lab entrance. We'll leave in about ten minutes."

* * *

I don't know how fast I made it to the dock, but it was a lot quicker than ten minutes. I hurried back to my room, slapped on some suntan lotion, grabbed my hat and sunglasses, and then half-ran, half-skipped to the lab entrance and across the road.

I couldn't believe I was going to spend a whole morning with a drop-dead knockout like Linda. Already I imagined that she saw beyond our superficial age difference and had been smitten by my intelligence and volleyball prowess. This could be the best day of my life, the one that would forever slay my awkwardness with girls. In fact, forget about girls. What I needed was someone more mature. Someone like Linda.

At the dock I spotted her down next to a fourteen-foot skiff with an outboard engine. Even better, I saw that she'd slipped off the white short shorts and stood in the full glory of her bronze bikini.

Then my fantasies came to a screeching halt. Linda wasn't alone. Sitting in the boat with her were Rod and another guy I didn't recognize. Served me right for getting my hopes up.

I considered going back to the barracks, but good sense prevailed. After all, a morning with Linda, even with two other guys around, beat picking grits out of my teeth or even looking at coin books. I bucked up my attitude and walked down the ramp to the skiff.

"Here he is," Linda greeted me, flashing a peppermint smile. My chest pounded. "Do you know Rod and Jeremy?"

"Hi." I shook hands with the shorter, stouter guy, Jeremy. He wore his greasy, shoulder-length black hair in a ponytail and had on a T-shirt for some band I'd never heard of called ZZ Top. I also nodded a hello to Rod who, I noticed, still wore the string of beads around his neck.

"Climb in," Linda told me.

I stepped over several buckets filled with hand nets, masks, and snorkels and perched myself on the middle bench, facing forward. Three pairs of flippers lay in the bottom of the boat.

Jeremy lowered the outboard's prop into the water, flipped the on switch, and pulled out the choke. The first few times he tugged the starter cord, the engine didn't want to turn over. After he pushed the choke back in, the outboard caught on the first pull. A cloud of blue white smoke wafted over us.

"Where are we going?" I shouted as we sputtered away from the dock.

"There's a sand island called Cormorant Island about a mile offshore," Linda shouted back. "Sometimes we find seaweed on the sandy bottom, and when we're lucky, we find little rock outcroppings with anemones and other invertebrates on them. We're hoping to collect some stuff for your dad's class there."

"Are you in his class too?" I asked, turning around to Jeremy.

"Yeah," he said, gunning the throttle. "Beats workin' for a livin'."

Whatever that meant.

Jeremy guided us through a few big waves as we motored around Fort Henry, an old brick fort that shared the east end of Shipwreck Island with SCUM-Lab. I'd noticed the fort when we'd driven in the night before. Now I pointed to it and asked, "What's the story on that?"

"Fort Henry," Jeremy answered. "Old Civil War fort."

"It was actually built earlier, but it played a big role in defending Mobile during the Civil War," Linda added.

"Can you go in there?"

"Sure. It's a state park now, but it's in pretty bad shape," Linda said.

Past the fort we moved out into the Gulf of Mexico, and the sea settled down to a tame foot-high swell. I turned my face into the wind, enjoying the sunshine and the gentle pounding of the hull against the waves. Linda sat in the bow, her brown hair blowing around her face and her long, tan legs stretched out toward me. The smell of her coconut-scented suntan oil wafted back to me on the breeze, filling my nostrils like a high-octane love potion.

"Have you been to Shipwreck Island before?" she asked, interrupting my worship.

"Uh, this is my first time," I said. "Usually my dad's in Pensacola during the summer."

"Oh, I know. I've taken two other classes from him."

"You're from the University of West Florida?" I asked, surprised.

"Yeah, not like these Alabama rednecks," she joked, motioning to Rod and Jeremy.

"A Florida cracker shouldn't be bragging," Jeremy said.

"Even a sexy one," Rod added.

I, of course, had also been thinking lustful thoughts about Linda, but Rod's remark struck me as out of line. Linda ignored it.

"Your dad's the best," she continued. "Before I took his biology class, I was in psychology. He inspired me to switch majors. Now I'm planning to get my PhD in marine science."

"That's great," I said, wishing I could think of something halfway intelligent to say.

Glancing past Linda's perfectly sun-browned shoulders, I spotted a large ship anchored to the southwest. Squinting, I could just make out divers bobbing in the water next to it.

"What are they doing?" I asked.

Linda turned her head, grasping her hair to keep it from blowing into her face.

"Those are the big treasure hunters," Jeremy said from behind me.

I looked back at him. "What do you mean 'treasure'?"

"They're diving some kind of wreck," Rod said.

"Wreck?"

"It's supposed to be a sunken Civil War ship," Linda

explained. "Those guys claim they're archaeologists looking for artifacts from the war."

"Yeah, right," said Jeremy. "That's what they're telling everyone. Rumor has it the ship sank with a ton of gold on board."

"What kind of gold?" I asked.

"How many kinds are there?" Jeremy said, showing off his keen wit.

"I meant was it bullion, coins, jewelry...what?"

"I heard it was coins," Rod said.

This was getting interesting. "Spanish? British?"

Rod shrugged apathetically. "Who the hell knows?"

"You sound like you know something about coins," Linda said.

"A little," I admitted, not wanting to come off as a coin nerd. A lot of people thought that coin collecting was only for little kids or pathetic old geezers with nothing else to do. But before I could say more, Jeremy called, "Here we are."

I shifted my gaze to a low sand island ahead of us. Sea oats and reed grass covered the center of the island, and flocks of gulls, terns, and pelicans crowded the shore. Despite the island's name, I didn't spot a single cormorant anywhere.

When we were about fifty yards away, the birds all took flight in a shrieking, swirling mass, and Jeremy killed the motor. Linda picked up a twenty-pound Danforth anchor from the bow. Her arm muscles bulging impressively, she tossed it into the water with a deep *kerplunk*. After playing out some rope, she tied it off on one of the boat's bow cleats. I looked down into the water and could see the rippled, sandy bottom five or six feet beneath us.

"It's unusually clear today," Linda observed. "We're lucky it hasn't rained for a couple of weeks. The mud from Mobile Bay can cut visibility down to a few inches."

"You're the boat tender," Rod told me as if someone had appointed him my boss. "If there's any trouble, fire off this air horn. We should be able to hear it underwater."

He handed me a can with a plastic horn attached to it. "Don't waste it," he added. "There's only so much inside."

"Aye-aye, captain." What did he think, that I was as dumb as Jeremy?

Rod removed the beads from around his neck and set them on the boat's middle bench seat. The three of them donned their masks and fins and one by one they rolled backwards over the side. I admired Linda's sleek form as she splashed into the water and paddled smoothly away, trailing a mesh diving net behind her. Then I sat back and sweated.

While the boat gently rolled in the waves, I scanned the sea surface and Cormorant Island for wildlife. On the other side of the island, terns and seagulls worked windrows of sargassum weed here and there, hoping to snag small fish or other morsels from the sea surface. About half a mile off I saw a huge manta ray leap out of the water. Other than that, nothing.

I noticed that a couple of inches of seawater had found their way into the bottom of our boat, so I picked up a plastic scoop and bailed most of it overboard. Then I turned my attention to the salvage ship. It looked to be about a mile away, and I wished I'd brought binoculars, because I couldn't see much of what they were doing. Every once in a while a diver popped to the surface and handed something up to the guys on deck. They also muscled a big white tube around in the water. I guessed it was some kind of dredging device to suck up sand from the bottom.

It'd be cool to look around on that boat, I said to myself. Just the thought of finding gold coins—and historic ones at that—made my nerves spark. Heck, I didn't even own a gold coin and figured I never would—not until I grew up and made scads of money.

"Yeah, right." I chuckled out loud. Money was something I'd probably never have—not scads of it, anyway. I'd most likely end up a poor biologist just like my father or do something else interesting but impoverishing. Still, the treasure bug stuck in my mind, and I promised myself I'd find out if there was any way to get on that ship.

Half an hour later Linda, Rod, and Jeremy made their way back to the boat. They handed up their nets, fins, and goody bags full of sea critters. Then I reached down and helped Linda back over the side.

"How was it?" I asked.

"Could've been better," she said, pulling off her mask. "I saw quite a few stingrays and some fish, but not much we could bring back. What about you guys?"

Jeremy also took off his mask and blew a plug of snot

from his nose. "Same here. A couple of slender starfish and a moon snail was all."

He handed me the round-shelled snail. The animal, heavy and dense in my palm, reminded me of a baseball.

"That was about it for me too," Rod said, rubbing water out of his eyebrows, "except for this guy." He reached into his mesh bag and pulled out an animal from before the age of the dinosaurs. Its hard, hinged shell, about a foot across, made it look like a little low-profile tank. A sharp, pointed tail stuck out eight inches behind it like one of those antennas for remote-controlled cars or planes.

"A horseshoe crab!" I exclaimed.

"Yeah. Your dad's going to be happy with that guy," Linda said. "It's the first one we've caught this summer."

The three of them filled the buckets with seawater and dumped the crab and other animals in. I pulled up anchor and Jeremy started the motor. As the boat eased forward, I sat in the bow looking back. Linda was perched on the bench seat near Rod and Jeremy.

"What are you going to do with the animals?" I asked her.

"Probably dissect them or put them in the live tank," Linda answered. "Your dad has found parasites in a lot of them."

"Yeah, that was his dissertation topic," I said. "Parasitic copepods."

The conversation lagged while Jeremy and Rod popped open cans of beer and Linda drank from her water bottle.

Rod finished his beer quickly and opened another one,

rarely taking his eyes off Linda. He looked like a five-year-old staring at a big piece of birthday cake. Then he said, "I really like your bathing suit."

"Thanks," Linda said flatly, and turned her gaze out toward the open water.

"I do too," said Jeremy, one hand on the outboard's throttle. "What's that string in front for?"

Her bathing suit top was tied with a little string bow. The bottoms were held on by two identical bows, one on each hip.

Linda glanced down. "It's just how you keep everything in place," she said.

"They look pretty flimsy," Rod said, winking at Jeremy. "Aren't you afraid they'll come untied?"

Linda casually returned her eyes to the ocean. "No, not particularly."

"But couldn't they just, y'know, work themselves loose?"

"It hasn't happened so far." From her voice I could tell she was growing tired of the conversation. Maybe even annoyed.

I thought Rod would get the hint, but he persisted. "What if someone just grabbed the end of this knot"—he reached over and actually touched the dangling end of the tie on her top—"and gave it a quick tug? What would you do?"

Linda didn't even flinch or slap his hand away. She just stared straight at him, her voice calm and steady, and said, "I wouldn't do anything."

Jeremy grinned at Rod. "Why not?"

"Because," Linda said, "neither of you boys would have the faintest idea what to do with a real woman."

The laugh escaped my throat before I could swallow it. Rod scowled at me and, even in the glare of the hot sun, I could see his cheeks redden. Talk ground to a halt after that.

Near my feet, however, I noticed Rod's beads wafting back and forth in seawater that had again collected in the bottom of the boat. Rod had obviously forgotten about the beads and couldn't see them from where he was sitting. On impulse, I picked up the plastic scoop and began bailing water over the side. Then, when both Rod and Jeremy were looking away, I scooped up the beads and quickly chucked them over the side, my heart pounding wildly.

Back at the dock, I climbed out first and the others handed the buckets and gear up to me.

"Hey, anyone see my beads?" Rod asked.

"What did they look like?" I asked.

"You know. The ones I was wearing."

"Didn't notice them."

"Did they fall into one of the buckets?" Linda asked.

I made a show of checking the buckets. "Nothing in here."

Jeremy and Linda both looked around the boat.

Rod swore and fixed me with an accusing gaze. "I took them off right before we went into the water. You sure you didn't see anything, Mike?"

I shook my head and tried to look innocent. "Nope."

"Maybe they got tangled up with one of the dive bags," Linda suggested. "I lost a pair of earrings that way once."

Rod looked like he wanted to hit somebody. "Yeah. Maybe."

We finished unloading and then began making our way back to the lab. Rod and Jeremy walked ahead, lugging the buckets of animals, while Linda and I followed thirty feet behind them, carrying the gear.

"I'm glad you came along today," Linda murmured.

I figured she was talking about the bathing suit incident. "Did...they bother you?"

She pulled her damp brown hair to one side. "Those clowns? Naw. Still, I appreciate you coming along."

It suddenly dawned on me that maybe that was why Linda had invited me in the first place—not because I was cute or good at volleyball, but to be a kind of chaperone. The thought depressed me. *Who am I kidding?* I thought. *Why would a woman Linda's age take an interest in a fourteen-year-old?* It was a dumb idea to begin with, and the more I thought about it, the dumber it seemed. But shoot, if being an escort got me more time with one of the most beautiful women on earth, was that so bad?

As we neared the lab Linda stopped. "By the way, I saw what happened to the love beads."

My mouth went dry. "You did?"

"Yep."

"And?"

"And I think it's an important lesson. On a boat you always have to make sure your gear is properly stowed."

I grinned. "Yeah."

She leaned over and kissed me on the cheek. "See you later."

I stood there speechless, watching her go.

Chapter 4

By the time I got to the mess hall my dad was walking out the front door. "Hey," he called. "I just finished lunch. You have a good time with Linda?"

"Yeah. It was…interesting."

"I'll bet. You catch anything worth keeping?"

"A few things. They took them to the wet lab."

"Good timing. We've got lab all afternoon. The students are just getting started on their research projects."

"Oh."

"Well, I've gotta run. You okay until dinnertime?"

I nodded, but even though I'd enjoyed going out on the boat with Linda, I could feel a twinge of anger in my chest. It was just like my dad to totally abandon me on my first full day here. How hard would it be to invite me to hang out with him in the lab?

He said, "I saw Kyle in here earlier. You could do something with him."

It was a typical suggestion from him—one that showed how clueless he could sometimes be as a father. I reacted appropriately.

"I'll be alright," I muttered, jerking open the mess hall door a little more forcefully than I needed to.

Our eyes met for a moment, and I thought he might at least ask if something was bothering me. Wrong again.

"Okay," he said as he hurried away. "Catch you later."

"Yeah."

After finishing lunch I was still feeling a bit steamed, so to get my mind off of my dad I went back to my room and dug out my coin books. During the year my dad always tossed his spare change into a two-liter lab beaker, and one of the highlights of my summer was to search through what he had saved. I spread my coin albums on my bed, dumped out the entire beaker full of coins, and eagerly plopped down next to them.

I had always loved hunting through change like that. I started collecting coins when I was only five, and I remembered the thrill of finding silver Mercury dimes and Franklin halves and even the occasional buffalo nickel. I used to hold an old coin in my hands and wonder about all the people who had held it since it was minted. A Standing Liberty quarter might have been in the pocket of a soldier at Pearl Harbor. An Indian head penny could have been spent to see Buffalo Bill's Wild West Show.

Now, of course, I rarely found anything very old, but I still enjoyed the hunt. And I still got lucky every once in a while. Picking through the coins my dad had saved, I scored a half-dozen 40-percent silver Kennedy half-dollars and two 90-percent silver halves from 1964. I also found a 1938 nickel, a silver 1958 Roosevelt dime, and a 1920 penny that was in better condition than the one in my collection. As a matter of principle, I set aside all of the wheat ear pennies—those minted before 1959. Recently they'd started to disappear from change, and I'd begun to hoard them. After about an hour of sorting and searching, though, the hot, humid air of the room caught up with me. My eyelids drooped, my head sank down into my pillow, and I fell asleep to the drone of the "swamp cooler" air conditioner in the window.

* * *

When I woke up I crawled off the bed and peeked through the ancient yellowed blinds at the outside world. The full fury of the Southern afternoon sun blasted my eyes like one of those death rays from *Star Trek*.

"Geez," I muttered, jerking back. "I surrender."

Still groggy, I stumbled through the bathroom to my dad's room to check the clock: 3:45 p.m. Dinner would be served at five, and I calculated that if I got my butt in gear I could squeeze in a run. I rummaged through my gym bag and pulled out my workout clothes and the new blue velvet Adidas running shoes my mom had bought me before I left California. After getting changed I gulped down a few swigs of water from the bathroom tap and made my way to the back fire escape.

The moment I stepped onto the metal stairs the heat hit me with a sucker punch. It was way too hot to run, but I knew I'd be too full after dinner and I wanted to stay in shape during the summer. I'd done okay in cross-country last fall, finishing third in one meet and fourth in another, but I wanted to improve this year. After stretching in the shade of the barracks, I took a deep breath and headed out.

Right away I wished I'd brought my sunglasses and hat. Even with the sun sitting lower in the sky, it felt like a laser beam cutting through my head. So much light reflected off the oyster shell parking lot that I had to narrow my eyelids to paper-thin slits just to find my way out of the lab gates. Things weren't any better when I reached the main road.

Like most Gulf Coast barrier islands, Shipwreck Island stretched long and skinny from east to west. Its main road aimed as straight as a rifle barrel for two miles without a single curve, from SCUM-Lab to the village in the center of the island. The pines and oaks along the sides of the road offered wisps of shade as I ran, but the hundred-plus-degree heat boiling off the black pavement canceled the trees' meager benefits. After only ten minutes my chest heaved, rivers of sweat stung my eyes, and—as an added bonus—it felt like someone was hammering an iron spike into my side.

Of course that's when the rednecks showed up.

Rednecks are supposed to drive beat-up old pickup trucks, but these guys skidded to a halt in a sky-blue convertible Corvair. There were three of them, all maybe seventeen, eighteen years old, and as they hopped out of the car, I tried to run around them.

No luck.

"Jes' where ya think yore goin'?" one of them demanded, blocking my way. He only stood a couple of inches taller than me, but his 190 or so pounds made him seem much more intimidating. His sweat-soaked brown hair stuck out like a rat's nest, and even from five feet away I could smell a chemical cloud of beer fumes—Lucky Draft, I deduced from the empties piled in the Corvair's backseat.

"Yeah," another one asked, splattering a stream of brown tobacco juice at my feet. "Whaddaya doon'?"

I know people often exaggerate Southern accents, but I swear, this second guy's drawl was so thick, he sounded like a distressed cow moaning. Taking an educated guess at what he'd said, I muttered, "I'm out for a run. See you later."

I made a move to go around again, but the first guy planted a meaty hand against my chest. "Hold up. We ain't done here."

"What do you want?" I said, hoping I sounded more courageous than I felt.

"Whadda *we* want? Why, hell, boy. This here's our island. The question is, whadda *you* want?"

I paused, debating if I should just make a run for it. Chances were these guys were too drunk to catch me. Then again, the island was long and straight. Where would I go?

"I'm down at the lab," I told them. "For the summer."

"Whoo-hoo!" the third guy said, his eyes redder than fresh liver. "College boy, huh? And I bet yore one 'a them Yankees too!"

Geez, I thought. *How long has this island been inbreeding?* "No," I told him. "My dad works at the lab."

Evidently this information bounced in and out of their heads totally unimpeded by brain matter, because the first guy said, "Well, then, college boy. Looks to me like you could use some—"

"Hey, fellas," a familiar voice said. "What y'all up to?"

My head whipped around to see Kyle Daniels straddling a Schwinn bicycle with a chipped green paint job.

The guy chewing tobacco slurred out a couple of garbled syllables, but Kyle had no trouble understanding him.

"Kyle," he responded. "Kyle Daniels. Who're you boys?" His easy manner seemed to throw the trio.

The one with his paw on my chest said, "You'd best butt out. This ain't none 'a yore business."

Kyle gave them one of his dazzling smiles. "'Course not, but ain't you boys got better things to do than work out yore female frustrations pickin' on tourists?"

If I hadn't already been gasping for breath, my jaw would have dropped. Even at fifteen, Kyle was still a sight younger and smaller than the thugs in front of me. I couldn't believe he'd just said what he did.

"What?" The guy with the rat's-nest hair narrowed his eyes. "You lookin' for trouble too?"

"With you boys? He-ell no," Kyle said. "I jes' hate to see you wastin' your time here when you could be off chasin' women or somethin'."

Even though the grin stayed on Kyle's face, I detected an edge to his voice. He was joking, trying to keep things light, but he was serious too. It was almost as if—well, as if he was offering *them* a way to back out of the situation.

Rat's Nest stared at Kyle for a moment. I didn't know what the guy would do, but I could see the calculations behind his glassy eyes. Then suddenly he pushed his hand off my chest, shoving me back a step.

"Aw, you two pissants ain't worth our time."

The second one emitted another cow noise and shot more tobacco juice in our direction. Then all three of them climbed back into the convertible and, throwing gravel, pulled a U-turn and headed back down the road.

Astounded, I stared after them. "Uh, thanks," I said, turning to Kyle.

He waved his hand. "Hey, I've met guys just like 'em almost everywhere."

"You have?"

"Sure. My school in Birmingham's full of 'em. They ain't so bad really. Local boys lookin' after their territory. They get sober again, you might actually like 'em."

"But those jerks *weren't* sober," I countered. "How'd you know they were going to back down?"

Kyle shrugged. "I just figured they would."

"But what if they hadn't?"

He paused, then grinned again. "Then we woulda had to run like hell!"

I laughed and began to think that I'd misjudged Kyle earlier. "What are you doing here, anyway?" I asked as we started walking back toward the lab.

Kyle pushed his bike along next to me. "I saw you joggin' away from the lab, and I asked myself, 'Who's crazy enough to run in the middle of the day in June in Alabama?' I thought I'd see what you was up to."

"I'm glad you did."

"What *are* you doin' out here?"

I told him about running cross-country and track at school. "You go out for any sports?" I asked.

"Naw. My old man, 'fore he died, always wanted me to go out for football, but I never took to it."

"You mean that wasn't your father?" I asked, remembering the man sitting with Kyle at dinner the night before.

"Ray? He's my step-pop."

"Oh. Sorry."

"It ain't nothin'. I like him better'n my old man anyway."

I thought about my own stepfather and wondered if I liked him better than my dad. No, I quickly decided. But my father could get me plenty angry sometimes.

"So what course is your stepfather teaching?" I asked Kyle.

"Teachin'?" Kyle laughed. "Ray's the maintenance man. He got the job a few weeks ago when the old guy got fired."

Embarrassed by my mistake, I shut up for twenty yards or so. Then I asked, "How was fishing this morning?"

"Got a couple croakers. That was it. Be glad you didn't go. 'Sides, we saw you headin' out with Linda."

Crap, I said to myself, my embarrassment multiplied. I'd totally forgotten Kyle had gone fishing next to the fort. Our boat must have gone right by him.

Kyle didn't make a big deal out of it. He just whistled and said, "Man, I wish I'd catch somethin' like that."

"Something like what?" I asked, confused.

"Like Linda."

"Oh, right. Linda. Yeah, she's good-looking. But she's smart too."

Kyle looked surprised. "Is she? I didn't think a girl that foxy would be."

"She is," I said, feeling a strange need to defend her.

"Huh."

We walked a few more paces. Then, Kyle asked, "So, you wanna go tomorrow?"

My mind lingered on Linda. "Go where?"

"Fishin'. Since I didn't have no luck at the jetty, thought I'd give the beach a try."

I wondered why he'd want to do anything with me after I'd lied to him earlier. "You sure you want me to?"

He grinned. "He-ell yeah. Maybe you'll bring me some luck."

"Probably bad luck," I said. "But if you don't mind that, yeah, fishing sounds good."

Chapter 5

Early the next morning we walked past the swimming pool and volleyball net and then headed west along the beach. Kyle had our fishing rods, and I carried his tackle box and a bag of frozen shrimp in a bucket I'd swiped from my dad's lab. Kyle's little sister Annie walked barefoot twenty yards ahead of us, carrying her own pole and bucket, seemingly in her own world.

"Does she really like to fish?" I asked, nodding toward Annie. "Or do you just have to bring her along?"

"Shoot. She's the best fisherman in the family," Kyle answered. "If I don't take her fishin' most every day, she starts barkin' at me like a German shepherd."

Annie set down her pole, ran down to the surf line, and pounced on something in the wet sand.

"What's she doing?"

"Mole crabs," Kyle said. "They make great bait."

As we caught up with Annie I saw her toss an oblong gray crustacean about as big as a quarter into her bucket.

"Oh," I said, recognizing it. "We call those sand crabs in California. I never knew you could use them to fish."

"Pompano like 'em," Annie said matter-of-factly.

Kyle looked at me, eyebrows arched. "See what I mean? She knows what fish like to eat."

I was impressed.

Annie trotted ahead of us again.

"Doesn't she have any friends on the island?" I asked Kyle.

"Naw. She likes to hang around me mostly, or go off by herself to read books." He paused. "We move around a lot, and she ain't so good at making friends."

Kyle seemed protective of his sister, but he didn't act like he was doing her a favor by hanging out with her. He just seemed to feel it was his job as her big brother. It made me feel like a jerk for trying to avoid them earlier.

I followed them along the beach, watching Annie nail another half-dozen mole crabs.

"Well, this looks good," Kyle said, driving the butt ends of our poles into the sand. Behind us, rising above some low dunes, stood a weather-beaten three-story house with a strange-looking circular tower in one corner. I began rigging my line with a metal leader, two size-6 hooks, and a triangular two-ounce lead weight.

"Thanks for bringin' the shrimp," Kyle said, impaling half of one on his fishing hook.

"No problem. My dad caught about five hundred pounds of them on a class field trip last week."

"Must be nice. Your dad's a cool guy."

"You think so?" I asked.

"Yeah. He's been real friendly to me and my stepdad, unlike some other folks out here."

"Yeah, he's usually pretty cool," I admitted, feeling a little guilty for getting mad at my father earlier.

Kyle skewered a piece of shrimp on his second hook, then asked, "Hey, why's he call you 'Jed' anyway?"

"Uh…" I could have easily answered the question in California but, I realized, not here in Alabama. I tried to weasel my way around it. "It's just something we started when I first visited him in Florida."

"I get it. It's cause you figured all us dumb Southern rednecks talk funny and go by 'Jed' and 'Gomer' like they do on TV, right?"

Kyle had me sighted-in like a two-point buck in an open meadow. He let me hang there for a few seconds, and I waited for him to pull the trigger.

Instead he said, "He-ell, no big deal. You think we don't make fun of you Yankees too?"

"I'm not a Yankee," I objected. "I'm from California."

"If you ain't from the Confederacy, you're a Yankee, believe me."

I laughed. "Okay, you win. I'm a Yankee."

Kyle laughed too, and we each picked up our poles.

We spread out a little, wading up to our knees in the surf, and then cast out our lines. Usually the Gulf stayed pretty flat, but today a three- to four-foot break was rolling in. My dad had told me that a tropical storm was angling north near the Yucatan, and I figured that's where the big waves were coming from. I knew storms like that could inflict some serious damage, but I didn't get too excited about weather reports anymore. Every summer a steady line of tropical storms and hurricanes entered the Gulf of Mexico, but most of them fizzled out or made landfall hundreds of miles away. They were mainly just something to fill up the nightly TV news and make a few waves for bodysurfing.

Within a few minutes I felt something nibbling at my fishing line. I gave it a jerk, hoping to set the hook into a whopper, but again felt the line go slack. Kyle didn't get any action right away either, but I heard Annie yelp and looked over to see her hauling in a silvery fish about a foot long.

"Pompano," said Kyle.

"Why don't you use mole crabs too?"

Kyle grinned. "I do sometimes, but frozen shrimp are a lot easier to catch."

We gave it a couple more minutes, then reeled in our lines only to find the hooks bare. "Dang blue crabs get more bait than the fish," Kyle said. We rebaited our hooks and cast them out again. As Annie reeled in another pompano down the beach, Kyle planted his pole in the sand and walked over to me. He pulled out a pack of cigarettes.

"Want one?"

A lot of kids at my school smoked, but I'd spent most of my life trying to get my dad to quit. I shook my head.

"Don't blame you," Kyle said, lighting up. "Dumb habit."

I looked out toward the water, and my eyes focused on the salvage ship I'd seen the previous day.

"Hey, Kyle, you know anything about that ship out there?"

He exhaled a white plume of smoke. "The treasure hunters?"

"So you know about them?"

"Not much. I seen their crew down at the tackle shop in town. Ain't the friendliest bunch."

I reeled in some slack from my line. "Any idea what they've found so far?"

"I can tell you what they *haven't* found," said a raspy voice.

Our heads whipped around to see a tall man with white, wispy hair standing behind us. He wore a faded red fishing cap, and his pale blue eyes peered out from beneath bristling eyebrows. The skin on his face was the texture of ancient brown leather, and an unlit pipe dangled from the corner of his mouth. Despite his age he stood straight as a piling in his long-sleeved button-down shirt and faded blue seaman's pants.

"Mornin,' boys," he said with a gentlemanly drawl.

"Hi," I said.

"Good morning, sir," said Kyle.

"It's a fine one, isn't it?"

"You got that right," Kyle answered easily. I just nodded and began counting my teeth with the tip of my tongue.

"Pardon me for not introducing myself," said the man.

"Name's Anton Dubois the Third. And who might you boys be?"

Kyle dropped his cigarette and kicked sand over it. "Kyle Daniels," he said, holding out his hand. "Kyle Daniels the *First*."

Mr. Dubois let out a deep, crusty chuckle, aged by salt air, and shook Kyle's hand.

"Michael," I answered warily. I didn't know the guy, after all. He might have been a serial killer for all I knew.

"Pleasure to meet you both." The old man removed the pipe from his mouth and pointed the stem toward the Gulf. "I couldn't help hearing you boys talking about our treasure seekers out yonder."

"I was just tellin' Mike they ain't exactly neighborly," Kyle said.

"Do you know anything about them?" I asked the man, curiosity overcoming my reserve.

He shook his head. "Not a lot. But I have a fair notion of what they're after."

"I heard it was gold," I said.

"That's what I hear too," the man replied.

"Where's it from?" Kyle asked. "The gold, I mean."

Mr. Dubois placed the pipe back in his mouth. "Excellent question. You boys know about the fall of New Orleans?"

Kyle snorted. "Everyone knows 'bout that. We study it every year in school. Sometimes twice."

I'd never heard a word about it in California, but I kept my mouth shut.

"Well," the man began. "When Captain Farragut broke his way past Fort Jackson and Fort St. Philip early on the morning of April 24, 1862, he took control of New Orleans almost without a fight. It was the first major Union victory in the War between the States. Sadly, it would not be the last."

I wondered if the man was joking when he said "sadly." Even after several summers in the South I couldn't believe there were people who actually wished the Confederates had won the Civil War. I mean, I know the South suffered terribly, but did anyone really wish that slavery was still legal? Mr. Dubois, though, looked dead serious, and to my amazement Kyle seemed to agree. "That's the truth, ain't it," he said.

Mr. Dubois continued his story. "Of course the valiant citizens of New Orleans quickly set about destroying anything that might be of value to the Yankees. They burned ships, thousands of tons of cotton, and weapons factories. The loss of the city crippled the Confederacy's ability to fight—and perhaps changed the outcome of the entire war."

"What does that have to do with the treasure hunters out there?" I asked, impatient for him to get to the point.

"That's a mighty fine question, Michael, and to this day, no one can answer it for sure. But here's what I reckon. Before the war, the New Orleans Mint was a federal facility, run by the Union. When the war broke out and the South seized control of the mint, some reports state that the Union left behind half a million dollars worth of foreign gold and silver."

"I heard about that," Kyle said. "And the Confederates melted it down and made coins out of it."

I was amazed I'd never run across this story in any of my coin books.

"Very good, Mr. Daniels. The Confederate President Jefferson Davis most likely used a good quantity of those coins to buy guns and ammunition. But rumor's always had it that an added stockpile of Confederate gold coins went unaccounted for. You won't find this information in any textbooks—at least none that I'm aware of—but in these parts, stories have been passed down for generations. Some people say that a quantity of these coins—maybe a thousand or two—were still sitting in the mint the day the Union prepared to attack New Orleans."

"So what happened to the Confederate coins?" I asked, unable to contain myself. "Did the Union get them?" I glanced at Kyle and could see that he was as hooked by the story as I was.

"There's the rub, Michael. When the Union raised their flag over the mint, not an ounce of gold was found. It had simply vanished."

Kyle and I sighed at the same time.

"Many people say there never was any more gold at the mint," Mr. Dubois continued. "That all the talk of missing gold was simply wishful thinking by people who imagined it could have changed the outcome of the war."

"What do y'all think?" Kyle asked.

Mr. Dubois looked out toward the salvage boat. His weathered lips cracked into a faint smile. "Oh, I believe there was gold, all right. I'd bet my house on it. What I don't believe is that those boys out there are ever going to find it."

"Why not?" I asked, just as I felt a strong tug on my fishing pole.

"You got one!" Kyle shouted.

I glanced over at his pole and saw that it was bucking too. "So do you!"

Kyle's pole toppled over, and he ran to grab it before the hooked fish dragged it into the surf. A minute later we both pulled flapping white sea trout up onto the wet sand.

Annie came running to see. "Whoo-hoo!" she hollered and pounced on Kyle's fish to pin it down before it shook itself off the hook. I managed to get mine free without help, and we ran stringers through both fish. Only after we'd placed our catch into our bucket did I remember Mr. Dubois.

I looked around, but didn't see him anywhere. Then I spotted the trail of footsteps leading back over the dunes toward the tall, weather-beaten house with the strange-looking tower.

Chapter 6

Satisfied with our catch, we headed back toward the lab. "So, what did you think of that guy back there?" I asked Kyle.

He shrugged. "Regular old-timer. His family's prob'ly been here since before the Civil War."

"You think he knows anything about the gold?"

"Naw." Any interest Kyle had shown during the man's story had faded from his face. "If he knew where that gold was, you think he'd be livin' in that broken-down old house?"

"Oh yeah," I said. "Good point."

"He's just a first-class storyteller."

We walked in silence for a few minutes. "So," I asked, "what do you do back in Birmingham?"

"Do?"

"You know, when you're not in school and stuff."

Kyle scratched his cheek, where a few blond whiskers had started to grow. "The usual stuff, I guess. Watch the tube. Hang out with guys in my neighborhood. How 'bout you?"

"Pretty much the same. Me and my friends ride our bikes a lot. My life isn't all that exciting."

"You like it better here with your dad?"

I had to think about that one. "Well…my mom's great and all that, and I like it in California, but I guess I have more fun with my dad." *When he has time for me*, I thought.

"I figured. Ray knows more what I like than my real dad did. He lets me help him work on his truck all the time."

"Really?"

"Yeah," Kyle said. "Tune-ups, changin' the oil, stuff like that."

I was impressed. Cars were just one of a hundred areas where I felt totally inadequate.

"That stuff's easy. Last winter," Kyle continued, "Ray 'n me pulled the engine on an ol' beater he picked up somewhere. We was rebuildin' it when—" Suddenly Kyle stopped and said, "Well, would ya look at that?"

Annie and I also halted and followed Kyle's gaze.

About a hundred yards ahead, two figures emerged from a space between two sand dunes. We watched them kiss, and we could hear them laughing as they brushed sand off themselves and walked hand in hand toward the labs.

"Rod," I said. "With Professor Halsted's wife, Becky."

"I'll be danged," Kyle murmured. "What a pecker-wood."

I looked at him, surprised. "I thought Rod was your friend."

Kyle shook his head. "Maybe at first, but did you see him carryin' on with Becky at the volleyball game the other night? What a jerk."

"Oh. I thought since you were playing pool with him—"

"Naw. If I was Dr. Halsted, I'd rip that guy—" Kyle glanced at Annie and stopped himself. "Anyways, he's a bottom-feeder. Hey, you don't like him, do you?"

"Heck no." I told him about the bathing suit incident on the boat with Linda.

"That don't surprise me none," Kyle said. "They oughta kick that guy outta here."

"Well, Mrs. Halsted doesn't have to go along with Rod."

Kyle scowled. "Yeah, well…Dr. Halsted oughta kick her out too."

When we reached the barracks I asked Kyle what we should do with the fish.

"You hungry?" he asked.

Even though it couldn't have been past 10:30 in the morning, my stomach rumbled at the suggestion. "Yeah."

"Me too. You know how to clean fish?"

Kyle didn't say it in a superior way, but I felt my spine stiffen. "Of course I know how to clean a fish."

He grinned. "No offense. I just don't know what they teach you Yankees out there in California. Anyways, you get them fish cleaned, 'n I'll meet you at the kitchen in back of the rec room."

"Okay." I wasn't exactly sure what Kyle had in mind,

but I carried our two sea trout to the back of the barracks while Kyle walked Annie home.

I actually had cleaned fish before—lots of times. For my thirteenth birthday my dad had bought me a really nice scaling knife. I used it to gut, scale, and behead the two sea trout we'd caught. Then, locating an outdoor hose, I carefully rinsed the last bits of entrails from the fishes' body cavities. Cleaning fish was kind of gross, but it always made me feel manly in some strange, primitive way.

I carried the trout inside to the kitchen counter in the rec room. Kyle arrived moments later holding a brown paper bag.

"What're you going to do?" I asked.

He opened the bag and took out a lemon, a cube of butter, a shaker of garlic salt, a couple of potatoes, and a roll of tinfoil. "I don't know how *you* usually cook fish, but I find it works pretty good to bake 'em in foil. That alright with you?"

"Yeah, sure," I said, trying to sound as nonchalant as possible. Even though I'd caught and cleaned fish, I'd never cooked one in my life and was startled to realize that Kyle actually planned to make us a real lunch right then and there. After turning on the stove, he smeared both fish in butter, lemon juice, and garlic salt, and then chopped up the potatoes into half-inch cubes. He wrapped everything tightly in foil and popped the packet into the hot oven.

Half an hour later, we sat down to one of the tastiest meals I'd ever eaten.

"How'd you learn to do this?" I asked, my mouth stuffed with trout. "Cook, I mean?"

Kyle shrugged. "Guess it's just somethin' I picked up. Mom works a lot. So's Ray. If I want me 'n Annie to eat, I gotta cook."

"This tastes really great."

He laughed. "Yeah, but you didn't taste the screw-ups. You don't even want to know how many times I filled our trailer with grease smoke, or how many nights Annie and I ended up eatin' popcorn for dinner."

He finished off the last of his trout and asked, "So, what do you wanna do now?"

I belched, then crumpled the fish bones and skin inside the foil.

"Well...I could show you my coin collection."

I waited for him to laugh or put down the idea, but his eyebrows lifted in interest. "You collect coins?"

"Yeah."

"Me too!"

"*Really?*" This was too good to believe.

"Sure," he said. "I collect just as many as I need to buy somethin'."

Geez, I thought. *I walked right into that one.*

"You collect coins, for real?" he asked.

"Yeah," I answered with less enthusiasm. "Some."

"Let's go see 'em."

I studied his face to see if he was putting me on again. "You sure?"

"He-ell yeah."

We cleaned up the kitchen, then I took him upstairs to my room.

Kyle studied our apartment with interest. "I've never been in these apartments before. Not bad."

"They're okay. I get a room to myself at least, which is good because my dad snores like a hippo. Where do you live?"

"Since there's four of us, they gave us a little house. I think it used to be an officer's house or somethin'. It was one reason Ray took the job. Not that a ton of other offers was floodin' in."

This was the second or third time Kyle had hinted that his folks had trouble holding on to work, but I didn't want to butt into his business. Instead I pulled out my AWOL bag and removed the two coin albums and my copy of the *Red Book.* "This is just what I brought from California," I told him, laying them out on my bed. "I have a lot more at home."

Kyle opened the Lincoln cents book and studied the coins with more attention than I'd expected.

"What's this?" he asked, pointing to a row of pennies. "The *S* and the *D*?"

"Those are the mint marks," I explained. "They tell where the coin was made. They use *S* for San Francisco and *D* for Denver. If it doesn't have a mint mark, it's from Philadelphia."

Kyle kept his eyes on the book. "Y'know, I seen them marks before, but I never knew what they meant."

"There were mints in other cities too."

"I know. My family and me saw the one in New Orleans once."

"Yeah. New Orleans coins had an *O*. On old silver dollars you find *CC* for Carson City, Nevada."

"I'll be danged," Kyle said, truly sounding interested. "How long you been doin' this?"

"About eight years."

"And in all that time you still ain't found all these pennies?" he asked, referring to the empty slots in the coin album.

"No. Some coins are really hard to find." I flipped to the Lincoln cents section in the *Red Book*. "Take the year 1938. You can see here they minted more than 156 million pennies at the mint in Philadelphia, but only fifteen million at San Francisco. That makes the 1938 San Francisco pennies rarer—and more valuable."

"How valuable?" Kyle asked.

"It depends," I said. "If it's in good condition a penny can be worth a lot. These columns in the book show their value in different conditions."

Kyle examined the figures on the page. "So you're sayin' I could find a penny in my pocket change that might be worth"—he ran his fingers over the dates and stopped at 1909—"I might find a penny that's worth a hundred dollars?"

"Well," I said dubiously. "I don't know anyone who's ever found a 1909-S VDB in their change."

"VDB?"

"In 1909, they put the initials of the penny's designer on the back of the coin—VDB, for Victor D. Brenner."

"Okay, but anyhow, you're sayin' it's possible?"

"Yeah, it's possible," I said. "But the most valuable penny I've ever found looking through change is worth maybe a couple of bucks."

"Hey," he said with a grin. "That's a carton of cigarettes, ain't it? What are we waitin' for?"

Kyle had lost me. "What do you mean?"

"I mean let's go into town and get us some coins!"

Chapter 7

Since I didn't have a bike Kyle let me use his green Schwinn while he rode his sister's bicycle. Annie's bike was at least two sizes too small for him, and his knees bumped into the handlebars as he pedaled. Kyle didn't mind.

"Hey, Mike," he called as we panted down the long straight road to town, "we're just like those two guys with choppers in *Easy Rider*." Kyle took his hands off the handlebars and raised them up in the air like he was throttling a motorcycle.

I laughed. My mom hadn't let me see the movie, but I knew exactly what Kyle was talking about. There wasn't a kid in America who hadn't rocked out to the movie's theme song "Born to Be Wild" and seen the famous posters of Peter Fonda and Dennis Hopper looking cool on their souped-up mean machines

Despite Kyle's attempts at humor, the overhead sun and the 500-percent humidity soon had me struggling. I was overjoyed when a few low buildings came into view at the end of the long stretch of roadway. "Where's the bank?" I called to Kyle as we pedaled into the tiny village.

"There ain't no bank on the island," Kyle informed me. "But we can get some change at the Bait 'n Stuff."

I wasn't so sure about that, but I followed Kyle to the little market that advertised the homemade tamales.

As soon as we walked in, the barrel-shaped storekeeper called, "Hey, Kyle! How y'all doin' this afternoon? How's that li'l sister of yours?"

"She's fine, sir," Kyle responded, walking up to the counter. "Mr. D'Angelo, I'd like ya to meet my friend Mike. He's a Yankee, but don't hold that against him."

Mr. D'Angelo laughed and stuck out a giant paw. "Any friend of Kyle's is a friend of mine. Without you Yankees I doubt I'd be in bidness for very long. Every winter, lotsa Northerners head down here for the fishin' and the sunshine. So what kin I do you for today?"

I stood silent through this exchange. The way Kyle had become best friends with almost everyone on the island, I was surprised the chamber of commerce hadn't hired him to be their official spokesman.

"Well, sir," Kyle said, "my friend Mike here's interested in coins, and we was wonderin' if you got—" Kyle turned to me. "Mike, tell Mr. D what we're lookin' for."

"Um, I like to look through rolls of coins," I said, prepared for a quick rejection. To my surprise the storekeeper simply asked me what kind. "Um, pennies and nickels mostly," I answered, "but almost everything really."

Mr. D'Angelo spread his huge hands on the counter. "I always keep plenty of change around. I reckon I kin part with a roll or two." He winked. "Depends on how much cash you have."

I asked him for a roll of each denomination, pennies through half dollars, and he opened the cash register drawer and pulled them out.

"Anything special you lookin' for? You used to could find most anything 'round here. Not that long ago a fisherman paid me with six silver dollars."

My eyes widened. "You're kidding."

Mr. D shook his head. "I wouldn't lie. 'Course we ain't likely to get any more of those, but a lotta change passes through these beat-up hands of mine. I'd be happy to keep an eye out for y'all."

"That'd be great," I said. "I mostly look for anything before 1965. Do you know what wheaties are?"

He spread his arms and did his best to look offended. "What century you think I was born into? 'Course I know what wheaties are! Bet I get twenty, thirty of 'em a day."

"Really?" I said. "Would you save them out for us to look through?"

"It'd be my pleasure—long as you spread the word that I sell the best tamales in the state of Alabama. How 'bout I fix you up with a couple right now?"

"We just stuffed ourselves on white trout," Kyle told him, patting his stomach.

"I heard the trout was runnin' today. But I'll hold you boys to it later."

I counted out the money for the coin rolls and bought two large cola-flavored Icees. We went out in front of the market and perched on a concrete curb in the shade to drink them.

"I can't believe he just did that for us," I told Kyle.

Kyle took a big slurp of his Icee. "Mr. D's a good guy. He'll save them coins you asked for, too."

We sat there talking and sucking down the sweet, cold cola until the last drops rattled up the straws.

"You want another one?" I asked Kyle.

"Naw." He pulled out his cigarettes and lit one up.

"How do you get cigarettes, anyway?" I asked him. "Aren't you too young to buy them?"

Kyle shrugged. "I ask Ray to buy 'em for me. Or I get 'em out of vendin' machines."

"Ray buys you cigarettes?" Even though my dad smoked, I couldn't imagine him encouraging me to light up.

Kyle took a big draw and exhaled. "Yeah. He used to smoke when he was a teenager. He prob'ly figures he'd rather get 'em for me legally than have to bail me out of jail for shoplifting."

"Has he ever had to bail you out?"

"Well, no, not exactly." Kyle laughed. "But I did get caught once tryin' to steal some goldfish out of a pet store. It was for Annie's birthday. Ray had to come down to the store and talk to the owner."

"Did Ray get mad?"

"Naw. He just told me not to let my mother know and not to do it again."

"Ray sounds pretty cool," I said.

"Yeah. He's been around the block a few times. Knows not to sweat the li'l stuff. What about you? What's your stepdad like?"

It took me a moment to readjust my brain. My life in California already seemed far, far away.

"He's okay." I paused. "He's an accountant. I guess that's why my mom married him. For security. He makes good money. She knows he's going to stick around."

Kyle took another puff. "Not exactly like your dad, huh?"

"No," I said. "My mom and dad used to fight a lot. They got married when they were students, so money was always a problem. And my dad could be a little reckless at times. I remember once when I was in kindergarten he just went out and bought a new sports car—a Sunbeam Tiger. Boy, did they get into it after that."

Kyle chuckled. "See, I told ya. Your dad's cool."

"Yeah," I said. "But it's not so cool when other people are depending on you. He still ticks me off sometimes."

Kyle stubbed out his cigarette and stood up. "Well, get used to it, Mike. That's somethin' ain't never gonna change. Parents are people just like us—'cept for one thing."

"What's that?"

"They're even more screwed up than we are. That's why we gotta look out for 'em."

I laughed, but I could hear a ring of seriousness in his voice.

We'd just tossed our Icee cups into a trash can when we

heard voices behind us. We turned and saw two men walk-ing toward the store. They wore grease-stained work clothes and blue caps with the name *Reef Wrecker* on them.

Kyle nudged me. "Those guys are from the treasure boat," he whispered.

"You sure?"

"Yep. They all wear them blue hats. You were wantin' to know more about their operation? Here's your chance."

"Uh, I don't know…" But as the men approached us, I steeled my nerve. "Excuse me," I croaked. "Do you work on the salvage boat? The one just off the point?"

The man in front scowled. "The *Reef Wrecker*? What's it to you?"

If it'd just been me, I probably would've mumbled an apology and moved on. But Kyle's presence gave me extra resolve. "I was wondering if you could tell us what you've found so far?"

The second guy laughed and said, "Yeah, I'll bet you'd like to know that! You and everyone else from Pensacola to Pascagoula."

They started to walk into the store, but I ratcheted up my courage an extra notch. "Do you ever give tours of the boat or anything like that?"

The two men looked at each other, then let out a mean guffaw that clearly told me I was never going to get any-where near that boat. I was ready to let it go, but as the men stepped past us, Kyle muttered something barely audible.

"What'd you say, boy?" the first man asked, glaring at him.

Kyle looked him right in the eye. "Axles. I was lookin' at that boat trailer across the way and thinkin' its axles needed work."

The two men again glanced at each other. "Yeah right. You beat it outta here before we bust *your* axles."

I held my tongue until Kyle and I got back on our bikes, safely out of range of the market. Then I let loose a ripping laugh. "I can't believe you said that!"

"He-ell," Kyle said, "all we was doin' was asking some questions. They didn't have to be such jerks about it."

I obviously wasn't as upset as Kyle. Shoot, I felt proud I'd even *asked* them anything, never mind their response. "If they really are after gold coins," I said, "they probably want as few people as possible to know about it."

"It ain't like we're gonna try to steal anythin'," Kyle said, still fuming.

"Money is money, I guess."

"Yeah," he said, pedaling hard. "I guess."

Chapter 8

From that day on Kyle and I spent almost all our time together. In the mornings we took Annie fishing or rode down to the market to get tamales and coins. True to his word, Mr. D'Angelo had bags of coins ready for us, and Kyle had just about as much fun as I did searching through them. The circulating coins of southern Alabama, I discovered, offered richer rewards than California. I don't know if there were fewer collectors in the area or what, but I added several missing dates to my collections, and in no time Kyle was putting together some pretty decent starter sets of his own. It surprised me that he was so into it, but after Mr. D'Angelo found us a couple of Franklin halves and an Indian head penny, Kyle was hooked.

When we weren't poring through our collections, Kyle and I played pool in the rec room, pestered Louella and "Ev-o-line" in the mess hall, or just poked around the marine station. Once or twice I took Kyle and Annie to the wet lab—a one-story wooden structure that used to be the recreation building for the Air Force base. The lab people had run a pipe to pump in seawater from the Gulf and had set up various aquariums and tanks for live animals. The sand dollars, snails, starfish, and baby fish especially drew Annie, who seemed tuned in with every animal she encountered.

Except for our occasional visits to the wet lab, I didn't really see much of my dad. The summer classes at SCUM-Lab ran all day, with lectures or field trips in the mornings and lab work in the afternoon. We met up in the mess hall for dinner, though, and went out by the pool for the evening volleyball games. On Mondays and Thursdays my dad "hired" me to grade and record his class quizzes. I was happy to find that Linda Garcon usually had the top test score—and equally miffed to find that Rod scored almost as well. As much as I disliked the guy, I was forced to admit that he had more brains than I'd given him credit for.

Before I knew it, Fourth of July weekend rolled around. The lab threw a barbeque and homegrown fireworks extravaganza on a little sand island across from the docks, and I had a pretty good time lighting off bottle rockets and stuffing myself on hush puppies and boiled shrimp. Kyle missed the fun because his family had gone off to Mobile to stay with his aunt.

The next afternoon I was lying on my bed, sorting through some wheaties when I heard a knock on the door.

"Enter," I called, not getting up.

Kyle burst in. "Mike!" he shouted, not bothering with a hello. "You up for some fun?"

I was surprised by how glad I was to see him, but I also felt sluggish after the late-night Fourth of July celebration. "Depends," I told him. "Like what?"

"Get your Yankee butt off the bed and I'll show you."

I put on my sandals and shuffled after Kyle down the back fire escape. He led me across a sandy strip to a barbed-wire fence that separated SCUM-Lab from Fort Henry. When we came to a place where the fence was sagging, he held up the wire and motioned for me to crawl through to the other side.

"We're going to the fort?" I asked.

"Shhh. Keep it down."

I scrambled under the wire, then held it while he passed through.

The fort's entrance was about fifty yards to our left. But Kyle began walking to the right.

I trotted to catch up with him. "We're not going to the fort?"

"Mike, you worry too much. Yeah, we're goin', but not through the gate."

I'd been wanting to visit Fort Henry but had held off for some reason, maybe saving it for a day when my dad and I could go together. Now, though, I could feel the excitement of discovery building inside of me.

The first thing I noticed was that the fort wasn't a square, as I'd assumed, but a giant pentagon with massive brick bastions jutting out from each of its five points. I was surprised at just how close to the water the fort sat. At the southeast bastion—the one right on the water—we had to scramble down over piles of rubble where the sea had scoured out the fort's rock and brick foundation. Though I knew it was unlikely the damaged bastion would collapse at that very moment, I hurried past just the same.

We kept walking beyond the southeast bastion, following a wide, dry moat around the rest of the fort. As we approached the huge northwest bastion, I began to wonder if Kyle knew what he was doing. "Where are we going?"

Kyle grinned. "Right here."

After a quick glance around, he jogged down into the dry moat and clambered up the other side to a square opening in the bastion wall. I hesitated, then followed him. The opening met us at eye level and looked like it had once had a cannon sticking out of it. Someone had jammed two-by-fours into the empty space, presumably to block trespassers.

Kyle checked again to make sure no one was watching, then began pulling hard on one of the two-by-fours. It was stuck in there pretty good, but it gave way with the fourth tug. We didn't have any trouble removing two more, leaving a gap big enough to climb through.

"Give me a boost," Kyle whispered.

I locked my hands into a stirrup and lifted Kyle up and through the hole. Then he reached down and helped me up.

We found ourselves in a large musty room with a stone floor and brick walls and ceiling. In addition to four square holes in the outer wall that looked like they were for cannons, the builders had created several tall vertical slits, probably to allow marksmen to pick off anyone trying to attack the outer walls. An arched doorway opened onto a smaller, windowless room labeled "Magazine" where ammunition must have once been stored, while a spiral stone staircase led up to the roof of the bastion where an old cannon was mounted. On the far side of the room a long brick tunnel ran about ninety feet toward the fort's center, and I could see the glaring light of the sun at its end.

"C'mon," Kyle whispered.

"Kyle, where are you taking me?" I began nervously counting my teeth.

"Shhh. Hurry."

Half-expecting a platoon of armed guards to descend on us, I trailed Kyle through the tunnel until we emerged onto what looked like the fort's central parade grounds. From Linda and some pamphlets back at SCUM-Lab, I'd already learned that the fort had been completed right before the Civil War, and that the Confederate army had used it to defend Mobile Bay. After World War II it had served a bunch of different purposes—as a gunnery school, a National Guard base, and a Coast Guard station. Finally a few years ago it had been turned over to the state as a historic museum and opened to the public. Looking over the parade grounds, I saw several adults walking around with cameras. A family stood reading a booklet at one of the numbered signs that seemed to be part of a self-guided tour.

"Act natural," Kyle muttered. "Like we're tourists."

I realized I'd been hunched over like a cat burglar, so I straightened up and walked along next to Kyle.

"Now where are we going?"

"You'll see."

Kyle led me up a long, wide ramp onto the fort's ramparts. From there I could see why the military had chosen this spot for defense. With the cannons mounted here and another battery of cannons three miles across the water at Fort Morgan, they could easily prevent anyone from going in or out of Mobile Bay. I paused to read an interpretive sign, but Kyle grabbed my arm and tugged me forward. At the southeastern part of the fort a thick, rusted chain stretched across our path. Behind it a sign read,

DANGER: CLOSED AREA
This area of Fort Henry has been closed until
further notice due to structural weakness.
DO NOT ENTER—KEEP OUT!

Kyle casually stepped over the chain.

I hesitated.

"C'mon," Kyle reassured me. "I've been here before. We won't bother anything."

A tiny thrill ran through me as I cleared the chain and caught up to him.

As we continued along the ramparts we passed several places where the brick had caved in to reveal dark, ominous holes leading down to who knows where. Sea oats and other plants grew out of thousands of cracks in the ramparts. Anoles—some people call them chameleons—scurried over the brick piles, and in one spot we saw a fat, venomous water moccasin lazily sunning itself.

Kyle picked up a brick.

"What are you doing?" I asked him.

"I'm gonna kill it."

I stepped in front of him. "No way. That snake isn't hurting anybody," I said.

Kyle reluctantly dropped the brick. "You Yankees really *are* crazy, you know that?"

On top of the southeast bastion, the one closest to the water, we came to another spiral staircase—this time leading down—and another warning sign not to proceed any farther. Kyle glanced around a final time and disappeared down the steps.

This staircase looked much more fragile than the one in the bastion we'd sneaked into, and as I took a step down I called, "Uh, this looks pretty iffy."

"Don't be a yellowbelly, Yankee," Kyle challenged, turning his face back toward me with a grin.

"Fine," I huffed and followed him down.

We descended into a large room identical to the one in the northwest bastion, but with two important differences. The first was that all the gun-slits and other openings to the outside had been bricked in, giving the chamber a dark, dungeonlike feel. The only light entering the chamber filtered down through the stairwell opening and through a hole at the far end where the brick had fallen in. The second difference was even more dramatic: For at least half of its depth the entire chamber had somehow filled with white beach sand.

"What happened here?"

"Don't exactly know," Kyle said. "I figure maybe storms or hurricanes washed all this sand in here 'til they finally decided to close up the openings to keep any more from gettin' in."

That made sense to me, but it didn't ease my anxiety. Trails of tiny footprints—from rats, no doubt—criss-crossed the sand. I felt a chill down my spine. Snakes, tarantulas, sharks, bats—I had no problem with any of them. But I hated rats. And I suddenly understood why that water moccasin had looked so fat and happy.

Even more alarming, I saw that dozens of bricks and chunks of mortar had fallen onto the sand from the decaying ceiling above.

"Let's get out of here," I said, glancing up to make sure another brick wasn't about to bash my brains in.

"What's the hurry? I like this place and besides, it's nice and cool in here."

I had to give him that. Insulated by the five-foot-thick brick walls, the air felt at least twenty degrees cooler down here than it did outside. Grudgingly I sat down on the sand next to Kyle and kicked off my sandals. Through the thick walls I could faintly hear, or feel, an occasional wave crash onto the rubble outside.

To get my mind off the rats, I asked Kyle, "How'd you find this place anyway?"

He shrugged. "Before you got to the island, I spent a lot

of time just snoopin' around by myself. Once, I decided to see if I could sneak in through that hole in the bastion and I stumbled across this here room. I kinda forgot about it again until we were drivin' back from Mobile this morning."

More relaxed now, I studied the walls and ceilings of the chamber. "Kyle, look at this brick."

"Yeah, amazin', ain't it? It's one reason I like comin' in here."

All around us the bricks had been fitted together with remarkable skill. Most impressive were the ceilings, which were made of delicate joining arches, like you might find in a Persian mosque or something. To keep them from collapsing, the masons had carefully cut and almost woven the bricks together, somehow mortaring them in place. I knew as much about architecture as I knew about the mating habits of elephants in Africa, but even I could appreciate the incredible craftsmanship surrounding me.

Kyle whipped out his cigarettes and lit one. Since that first day fishing he hadn't offered me one, but now, for some reason, he did. I reached over and took the lit cigarette from him.

Kyle grinned. "Gonna dance with the Devil?"

I shrugged. "I just want to see what the big deal's about."

I put the cigarette between my lips and inhaled. The smoke felt mellow and smooth in my lungs—for about three seconds. Then my throat and lungs caught fire. I tried to keep down the urge to cough, but my entire body convulsed and I lurched forward, thrusting my feet into the sand.

"I shoulda told you not to inhale right away." Kyle chuckled, obviously enjoying my predicament.

"Th-thanks a-a-lot," I coughed, again heaving forward.

I kept hacking for over a minute, my eyes full of tears and my body flushed with exertion. Finally, though, I managed to get control of myself.

And that's when I felt the metal object pressing against my toe.

Chapter 9

I handed the cigarette back to Kyle and carefully reached into the sand for the mystery object. At first I figured it must be an old beer can or a rusty nail, but I pulled out the last thing I ever expected—a slightly tarnished golden disk about an inch and a half across. I knew instantly what it was—or what it was supposed to be. At first my mind told me that it had to be a counterfeit, like one of those plastic coins you get for prizes at fairs or carnivals. But feeling the weight of the coin in my hand, my heart started to pound and tiny needles of nerves stabbed my skin.

"Whatcha got?"

I stared at the object. Stamped onto the disk was an image of Liberty I'd studied hundreds of times in coin books. I never imagined I'd be holding it in my hands.

"It's a coin," I croaked. "A gold coin."

"No bull?" Kyle scooted closer to get a better look. "What kind?"

As I flipped the coin over, I started to explain that it

was a twenty-dollar gold piece—a "double eagle." Instead of finishing my sentence, though, I read the words on the back of the coin. "Holy crap!"

"What? What is it?" Kyle pressed, scooting closer.

"An 1861 double eagle," I said. "From the New Orleans Mint."

"Lemme see that." Kyle reached over and took the coin from my trembling fingers. He turned it over and hefted its weight in his hands. "Dang. A gold coin. You ever seen one before?"

"I've seen gold coins in coin shops, but—"

"Hold on a minute!" Kyle said, studying the coin. "On the back it says 'Confederate States of America.' I don't remember seein' these in the *Red Book*."

"They're not."

"How come?"

I stared straight at him. "Because they don't exist."

He looked from me to the coin, then back at me. "Say again?"

"Kyle," I said, my voice almost a whisper, "in all the years I've been coin collecting, I've never heard of this coin."

"You mean it's a fake?"

"Let me see it again."

Kyle passed it back to me and I examined it more closely. The front of the coin, the obverse side, looked exactly like a regular double eagle, picturing an old-fashioned bust of a woman wearing a headband with the word "Liberty" across it. But the reverse featured a shield with some kind of twigs or branches on either side and what looked like a cap sticking out of its top.

"I don't know," I said. "It looks real, but it's probably just a gold token or a collector's medal made later. It might even be gold-plated nickel or lead or something. People like to collect memorabilia like that."

"That what *you* think it is?"

As I considered the question, one of my mom's favorite phrases popped into my head: If something seems too good to be true, it probably is.

"We need to do some research," I told Kyle. "Now."

* * *

When we got back to my room I went straight to my *Red Book*. I flipped through it page by page, checking the regular listings for double eagles as well as the miscellaneous sections in the back of the book.

"Look," I said, leaning over so Kyle could see. "In the back here, it says that at the New Orleans Mint, the Confederates minted four silver half dollars."

"Four different dates?"

"No. Four coins. Period. I guess they were tests or patterns or something like that."

Kyle took the book from me and studied the pictures. "The design on the back looks like the one on our coin."

"Yeah," I said, pointing to the description, "but it also says, 'Lack of bullion prevented the Confederate government from proceeding with any coinage plans that might have been made.' In other words, it doesn't say anything about any Confederate gold coins."

"So that means ours is a fake."

I shook my head uncertainly. "I don't know what to think about this. We need to talk to someone who'd know."

"Like who?"

"Well, back home, I'd go down to the local coin shop or maybe the library."

Kyle guffawed. "Good luck finding either one around here."

"Yeah, that's what I was thinking."

We sat there chewing over our predicament. "Wait," Kyle said, his face brightening. "When we were in Mobile, my mom left her purse at my cousin's house. She's plannin' to go back and get it tomorrow. Maybe we could hitch a ride."

* * *

The next morning I was already waiting out front of our building when Kyle's mom drove up in their bronze-toned '63 Buick. Annie sat in the front passenger seat reading one of the *Chronicles of Narnia* books. I climbed into the backseat next to Kyle.

I soon learned where Kyle had gotten his talkativeness and friendly manner. Mrs. Daniels chatted nearly the whole way to Mobile. She asked me a ton of questions about California, and then launched into a long history of the places they had lived. I learned that before living in Birmingham, the family had lived in Dothan, Tuscaloosa, and several other Alabama towns. I wondered again why they'd moved so often, but I didn't think it would be polite to ask.

As we entered the outskirts of Mobile I scanned the yellow page I'd torn from the SCUM-Lab office phone book earlier that morning. Under the heading "Coin Dealers," seven different shops were listed. A couple of the entries looked more like pawn shops, but I gave Kyle's mom the address of a likely-looking store downtown on Dauphine Street. She found the place without difficulty.

"I'll be back for you around noon," she said as we hopped out of the Buick. "I got to get back to work this afternoon, so y'all keep an eye out for me."

The coin store was located in a neat old building with a second-floor wrought-iron railing like the ones I'd seen in pictures of the French Quarter in New Orleans. The building looked pretty run-down, though. In fact, the entire downtown area around us looked strangely depopulated, like most of the people who had once lived here had up and moved somewhere else.

A buzzer sounded as we entered the shop, and a man stepped out through a curtained doorway in the back. His face sagged with age, and he wore a short-sleeved button-down shirt that looked like it hadn't been pressed since the Eisenhower administration. "Howdy, boys," he said as if we'd interrupted his midmorning nap. "What kin I do for y'all?"

"Just looking," I answered.

The man nodded. "Fine. Y'all need me, just holler." Then he disappeared back through the curtain.

"Thank you, sir," Kyle called after him.

The store reminded me of coin stores in California. It featured four or five display cases with rotating shelves. Each case had a pair of black buttons that you pushed to move the shelves forward or backward like a little Ferris wheel.

"These are cool," Kyle said, pressing the top button on the nearest case. I glanced into it and watched rows of buffalo nickels, Mercury dimes, and Standing Liberty quarters rotate by. Each coin was stapled or taped into a square cardboard holder with a round cellophane center to allow viewing. On the corner of the cardboard, the dealer had scribbled each coin's date and mint mark, condition, and price. "Look," Kyle said, pressing the stop button. "There's a 1916-D."

"Really?" I peered into the glass case. On the top shelf lay one of the key coins in the Mercury dime series.

Kyle whistled. "Man, that's a pretty coin."

The coin was listed in VG—Very Good—condition and was well-worn, with scratches and other contact marks on Liberty's cheek. I had seen better, but I still felt a thrill looking at it. Only 264,000 of these had ever been made. That sounds like a lot, but it was far less than any other Mercury dime. For collectors like me and Kyle, the 16-D was one of the holy grails of coin collecting.

"One hundred and fifteen bucks," Kyle said.

I sighed. "We can dream."

Kyle continued looking through the cases while I explored the rest of the shop. On the counters was the usual assortment of coin albums, books, and magazines. A long glass case was filled with proof and mint sets— annual sets of coins produced by the U.S. Mint especially for collectors. One corner of the store was devoted to a bid board where members could put up their own coins for sale. I glanced through the current offerings, but it mostly looked like the usual garbage people wanted to get rid of.

The owner reemerged through the curtain. "Y'all see anything that int'rests you?"

Kyle grunted. "Too much."

"Can I see this penny over here?" I asked, moving to one of the cases.

The shop owner walked around to the back of the case and unlocked it.

"Which one?"

"Top row, third from the left—or your right."

The man picked up the penny. "This one?"

"Yeah. I mean yes sir."

I wasn't really interested in the penny, but Kyle and I had agreed that we didn't want to bring up the subject of the gold coin directly. If by some miracle our coin turned out to be the real deal, we didn't want to set off any alarm bells.

The dealer handed me the penny, and I pretended to study it carefully. After a moment, I set it down on the counter in front of me.

"Say," I said, trying to sound casual. "We were just down on Shipwreck Island and saw a salvage boat out there. Someone said they were looking for gold coins. Do you know anything about it?"

He chuckled. "Heck yeah. Everyone knows 'bout that."

"What do you think they're lookin' for?" Kyle asked, sidling over.

The sag suddenly left the man's face, and I could tell we'd struck a topic of interest.

"Article in the paper a couple months back speculated they'd found the wreck of a boat called the *Skink*. Rumor has it the ship went down with gold coins from the mint in N'Orleans. Likely '61 double eagles."

"Why double eagles?" I asked, struggling to keep the excitement out of my voice. "Didn't the New Orleans Mint produce lots of different gold coins?"

The man slid onto a tall stool behind the counter. "It's like this," he began, his face growing more animated with every word. "The Union still controlled the N'Orleans Mint 'til January 1861. After that the state of Louisiana took over, but they still had a supply of gold, so they kept mintin' coins under the state's direction 'til April. That's when the Confederacy officially took over."

"And they kept makin' double eagles?" Kyle asked.

"A few," the man said, "but their gold ran out pretty quick. I think I read they only minted two, three thousand, somethin' like that."

"Could you tell who made which coins?" I asked. "I mean, if you looked at one of them, could you tell if it was minted under the Union, the State of Louisiana, or the Confederacy?"

The dealer smiled and slapped his palm on the glass case. "No sir! That's the thing. Both the state of Louisiana and the Confederacy kept usin' the Union coin dies."

"Dies?" Kyle asked.

"The molds they make the coins from," I told him.

"Why didn't the Rebs make their own?"

"I reckon they had other things on their minds, like winnin' the war," the man said, obviously pleased with his witticism. "Prob'ly didn't have no time to make new dies."

"So," I said, as if it had just occurred to me, "are you saying the Confederacy never minted gold coins using its own dies?"

"That's exactly what I'm sayin'. 'Course there's been rumors now and agin that they did, but it ain't in the records. As far as I know, ain't a single Confed'rate gold coin ever turned up." The man paused and looked straight at me. "Unless you know somethin' I don't."

I felt my throat tighten. Had I said too much?

As usual, Kyle saved me. "Yeah, right!" he said, whacking me on the back. "That's a good one, ain't it, Mike?"

I barked out a weak laugh. "Yeah."

The dealer's face broke into a grin. "Too bad," he said. "You find a coin like that, yore money problems are solved forever."

Chapter 10

bought the penny I'd been looking at and then asked the dealer if there was a library nearby. "Shore is," he said. "Central branch. Jes' up the street, and over on Gov'ment."

"Thanks," I said.

As we left the coin shop Kyle turned to me. "Why'd you want a library?"

"I thought maybe we could find some records of the ship the salvage guys are working on."

Kyle grinned. "You're pretty smart for a Yankee."

"Do we have time?"

"Are you kiddin'? My mama gets to talkin' with my aunt, it can go on for weeks."

As we headed toward the library I could already feel heat radiating up off of the sidewalk, and with the sun almost directly overhead I felt like we were under a gas-fired broiler. All we needed was some lemon juice and garlic salt on us and we'd be ready to serve.

"So, looks like you were right," Kyle said, wiping the

sweat from his forehead. "The Rebs never minted their own gold coins."

"Well, that man did say there were *rumors* they had," I replied. "Our coin could still be real."

Kyle looked doubtful. "You think so? You think they could've minted their own coins without anybody findin' one all these years?"

I shrugged. "Probably not. But what if they were all on that one ship and the ship got sunk?" My argument sounded as weak to me as it did to Kyle.

"Yeah, but then how'd the coin end up inside that fort?" he asked.

"The only way," I said slowly, "would maybe be if those guys on the ship had found the coins and then dropped one at the fort."

"But if they'd found the coins, they wouldn't just be carrying 'em around," Kyle countered.

I didn't have an answer for that one.

We crossed the street, relieved to reach the shadier sidewalks of Government Street. Kyle kicked at some acorns from the large oaks spreading overhead. Then, almost out of the blue, he asked, "Why do you think there weren't no other coins with the one we found?"

We both stopped and stared wide-eyed at each other.

I slapped my forehead. "Man, I can't believe we didn't think of that before!"

"Mike," Kyle said, "we gotta get back inside that fort."

"Right. But since we're here, I still want to hit the library, okay?"

Kyle swept his hand forward like a court jester. "You're the boss."

The Ben May Public Library was a huge, two-story white building with fancy columns and stately wings sticking off to either side. It filled the entire 700 block of Government Street. We joined a steady stream of people entering the library's main doors and followed the signs up the left-hand staircase to the reference desk.

"Allow me," Kyle whispered as we approached the desk. "Mornin', ma'am," he said, flashing the librarian a mouthful of white teeth.

"Why, good morning." The woman behind the desk had short blonde hair and wore oversized reading glasses that made her look like some hip kind of beetle. I guessed she was still young enough to be charmed by Kyle's manners and good looks. "How may I help you?"

"We'd like to find out about a Confed'rate ship called the *Skink*."

The librarian removed her glasses and bored into Kyle with her brown eyes. "Oh yes. The freighter they're salvaging off the coast."

"Yes ma'am. That's the one."

"There've been several articles in the *Register* this year. I don't believe they've been put on microfiche yet."

She led us to the periodicals section and showed us shelves containing back issues of the local paper. "I don't recall the exact dates of the stories," she said. "But you might start in February."

"Geez, look at 'em all," Kyle said as the woman left us.

"We're never going to make it through all these."

"Come on. Let's split them up. You take February and I'll take March."

We each took a stack of newspapers to a nearby table and paged through them one by one. After five minutes Kyle said, "Found it!" He held up a front page with the headline "Treasure Hunters Seek Sunken Civil War Fortune." Kyle spread the newspaper on the table and we read the article silently.

> Antiques Limited of Fort Lauderdale, Florida, has announced it will begin salvaging the wreck of a Civil War ship this spring. A Federal court granted the company exclusive salvage rights to the wreck after its discovery in the summer of 1972. The company has not disclosed the name, exact location, or contents of the wreck, but private experts suggest that the ship is the Confederate blockade-runner *Skink*.
>
> The *Skink* was sunk by Union warships in the spring of 1862 as it headed for Havana, Cuba. Until recently the ship was thought to have been lost off the coast of western Florida. According to experts, however, newly uncovered documents suggested a location closer to Alabama. These documents are thought to have helped lead explorers to the ship's remains.

> The wreck is rumored to contain a supply
> of gold coins from the New Orleans Mint, but
> an Antiques Limited spokesman maintains
> that the company is interested in the ship for
> "purely historic" reasons.

The rest of the article contained several quotes by an Antiques Limited spokesman and speculation about what the company would find. Several experts suggested the wreck contained coins or bullion, but no one mentioned Confederate coins specifically.

We finished reading the piece and were scouring other back issues of the newspaper when the beetle-eyed librarian returned.

"Did you find anything?"

"Yes ma'am," Kyle told her. "Right where you said it'd be."

"Oh, good," she said. "I decided to dig around to see if I could find anything else that might help you." She laid a large book called *Ships of the Civil War* on the table. "I thought this might have some information on the *Skink*, and sure enough, it did." She proudly slid her finger under a bookmark and opened the volume to reveal a black-and-white diagram of a long, low-lying ship with two smokestacks sticking out of the top. "The *Skink* was what they called a side-wheel steamer," she explained. "See how the paddle wheels are located on the sides of the ship?"

"Oh yeah," I said, studying the diagram.

"The paddle wheels were driven by a pair of steam engines, so she was probably pretty fast."

"Which would be what they needed if they wanted to escape Union warships," Kyle said.

"Perhaps," the librarian said, again removing her glasses.

"1862," Kyle said. "That's before the blockade was effective. They hadn't started buildin' blockade-runners by then, had they?"

"Well, that's my thought," the librarian told him. "I know the newspaper articles referred to the *Skink* as a blockade-runner, but I think she was just a regular fast freight carrier."

"Really?" I asked.

"Yes," the librarian continued. "According to this book, the specialized blockade-runners only started later, when British shipping companies began building ships specifically to evade and outrun Union warships."

"Yeah," Kyle said, pointing to the picture, "but look at her shallow draft. Even if she wasn't built to run the blockade, she's perfect for the job."

"That's right," the librarian said. "And that would be especially important for the shallow waters in and around Mobile Bay. She wouldn't sit too low in the water, even fully loaded."

I'd stayed mostly silent during this exchange, intimidated by my pathetic lack of knowledge of the Civil War—and impressed by how much Kyle knew. It was obvious he'd been holding out on me, but I wasn't surprised. He never showed off about anything.

"So," I said, struggling to wrap my mind around this new information, "if the Confederates wanted to sneak gold out of New Orleans before the Union invaded, this would be just the kind of ship they'd be looking for?"

The librarian nodded. "I would think so. The shallow draft would also allow it to sneak back into another Southern port such as Mobile, near where the treasure hunters believe it got sunk."

We all mulled this over for a moment, studying the diagram in the book.

"But here's what gets me," Kyle said. "Accordin' to that news article, this ship *wasn't* headin' toward Mobile. It was goin' to Havana. So how'd it get sunk here? You'd figure it'd go far out to sea to get around the Union blockade. Instead it's sunk right offshore, huggin' the coast. It don't make sense."

"Man, you're right," I said. "I didn't think about that."

The librarian shook her head. "I'm afraid I can't help you there, boys."

Kyle gave her another big smile. "That's okay. Thank you, ma'am, for all your help."

We hurried out of the library and back to the coin shop, where we found Kyle's mother pacing the sidewalk next to their Buick.

"Where've you boys been?" she barked, her face hot with worry. "Didn't I tell y'all to wait here for me?"

"Sorry, Mom," Kyle said.

"It was my fault," I told her. "We were at the library. I thought we'd have time to look up something."

Her face softened as she walked around to the driver's side door. "Well, no matter. But next time I don't want you boys wandering off like that, you hear?"

"Yes ma'am," we both answered, climbing into the backseat.

Chapter 11

B y the time Kyle's mom let us out by the mess hall, I felt like I had fire ants down my shorts. "How early do you think we can sneak back into the fort?" I asked.

Kyle looked up at the sun. It was about four o'clock and the fort wouldn't close for another hour.

"We should wait 'til all the people are gone. We go carryin' a couple shovels around, it's gonna look suspicious."

"Do you know if they have a night watchman?"

Kyle scratched his sideburn whiskers. "Hmmm... Don't think so, but I've seen the island police checkin' the place out now and then."

"Okay. You want to come by my place about seven or so, after dinner?"

"See ya then."

Kyle started to turn away from me, but I remembered something. "Hey, wait."

He stopped.

I reached into my pocket and pulled out the square holder with the penny I'd bought in Mobile. "Here."

He looked at it and then back at me.

"We needed to buy something," I explained. "I thought I might as well get something you were missing from your collection."

Kyle studied the coin. "1909 VDB, VF condition."

"Sorry it couldn't be the S-VDB," I joked, referring to the coin's much more valuable cousin.

He didn't respond, and for a moment I thought he didn't like the coin.

"Thanks, Mike," he muttered. "No one's ever..." He seemed about to say something else, but then he just nodded. "See ya later."

I walked back to the barracks, wondering about Kyle's reaction to the penny. When I'd first started spending time with him, Kyle had always come across as so relaxed and sure of himself, like his life was a breeze. But the more I got to know him, the more I felt like maybe things were harder for him than he let on. Like just now with the penny. Watching his reaction, my first thought was that no one had ever done anything nice for him before. I was sure that wasn't true, but it got me wondering. Maybe Kyle had a lot more on his shoulders than he ought to. Maybe he was strong because he had to be.

Climbing the stairs to our apartment, I shook my head clear and again focused on the issue at hand: the double eagle. The idea of finding more of the coins made my stomach flip. *If there was one,* I thought, *there's just got to be more.* I kept reminding myself that the coin was probably a fake, but that didn't stop me from figuring out what I was going to do with my share of the treasure.

When I pushed the door open to my room my fantasies were cut short. "Hey, Jed," my dad called. "That you?"

I walked through the bathroom to his bedroom. "Hi. What are you doing here?"

"Don't sound so enthusiastic," my dad joked. He was sitting at his desk scribbling on a lined yellow notepad, a cigarette burning in the ashtray. He put down his pen and pushed back his chair to face me. "After this afternoon's quiz, I decided to let my students have the rest of the day off," he said. "Everyone's been working hard, and besides, I need to plan the next couple days' lectures. How was Mo-beel?"

I flopped down on his bed. "It was good."

"You find a decent coin shop?"

"Pretty decent. I bought a penny for Kyle's collection."

"What kind?"

"1909 VDB."

My dad raised his eyebrows. "Isn't that like the crème de la crème of coins?"

I was surprised that he remembered. "No. You're thinking of the S-VDB."

"Still, that was a cool thing for you to do."

I shrugged, wondering for the twentieth time if I should tell my dad about the double eagle and the real reason we went to Mobile. For the twentieth time I decided to keep my mouth shut. It wasn't that my dad wasn't trustworthy or that I didn't *want* to tell him. It was just that Kyle and I still weren't exactly sure what we'd discovered. Besides, I wasn't sure I wanted to hear what he'd say about my sneaking into the fort and carrying off something I'd found there.

"Well, I'm glad it was a good trip," my dad said. "I'm also glad you're back. I need you to grade these tests for me tonight. I thought we could play a little cribbage afterward."

"Uh, well…" I stood back up. "Kyle and I kind of planned to do something tonight." By the time the words were out of my mouth, I was already feeling guilty—and a little angry at my dad too. Since my parents had broken up, my dad and I had made a nightly ritual of playing cribbage together when I stayed with him. Some of our best times were spent sitting around counting out points in cribbage, watching Johnny Carson on *The Tonight Show*, and just shootin' the bull. But this summer he hadn't had much time for me. In a way I resented how he just assumed I'd be available whenever *he* felt like doing something.

"Oh, I see," my dad said. "If you're too busy, I can grade these myself. It's just that you've been spending a lot of time with—"

"Wait a minute," I said, interrupting him. "*You're* the one who's always too busy. You can't expect me to just sit around waiting until you have a free minute." I knew my voice sounded more accusing than I'd intended, but I was tired of pretending everything was great.

My father just stared at me for a moment. "You're right, Mike," he said finally. "And I'm sorry."

But I wasn't ready to let this go. Suddenly a whole potful of frustrations came boiling to the surface—things I hadn't even known were there.

"I mean, what do you want?" I said. "You dump me out on this island all alone and then expect me to make new friends. When I do find someone, you expect me to be here whenever *you* want?"

"Well, no. I just thought—"

"You *didn't* think. You never do! If you wanted to see me more, why did you move all the way to Florida?"

By this time, tears were welling in my eyes.

"You always tell me how much you miss me and everything," I continued, almost shouting. "I used to believe it, but now I think you're glad I'm only here in the summers. You like it that you don't have to deal with me the rest of the year. I think that's why you moved so far away in the first place."

"That's not true," my father protested.

"It is true! I have to go back and forth every year, living with two different families. Do you think that's easy for me? Do you even think about it?"

My dad handed me a Kleenex, but I batted it away.

"Come on, son," my father said. "Sit down for a minute."

"No."

"Please. I want to tell you something."

"No!" I said and stormed out of the room.

* * *

After dinner the mercury dipped below 90 degrees, but my blood still boiled with anger, guilt, and a dose or two of confusion. I was relieved that I had Kyle and the fort to get my mind off of the fight with my father. While the students and faculty traipsed off to the volleyball court and the pool, Kyle and I slipped away. We each grabbed a shovel and a flashlight from the maintenance shed and made our way toward Fort Henry. Kyle noticed my silence as we walked.

"You okay, Big Mike?" he asked.

I shrugged. "I got into a fight with my dad."

"What? He bawl you out for going to Mobile?"

"No. It was nothing."

"Yeah, I know what that's like," he said. "My mom and me have fought over nothin' more times than I can count."

I felt grateful that he let it drop.

We reached the barbed-wire fence at the edge of the fort and paused, our eyes scanning ahead. Not a single car occupied the long gravel parking lot, so Kyle and I crawled through the wire and hurried directly to the bastion where we'd sneaked in before. Within seconds we were inside.

In the evening gloom the fort seemed a lot eerier than it had at midday. When we entered the long tunnel that led to the parade grounds, Kyle turned on his flashlight. As the beam played against the wall, I noticed the letters "E*BLANC" stamped into some of the bricks.

"Look at these letters," I called to Kyle. "You think this is the name of the brick company?"

"Could be," he said. "I'll bet they used slaves to make 'em back then."

I reached out and ran my fingertips lightly over a brick's glazed surface, tracing the outline of the letters. I shivered. For a moment, it seemed that history was reaching out and pulling me close. Too close.

"Mike, what're you doin'?" Kyle was already way ahead of me.

"Nothing," I said, hurrying to catch up.

We exited the tunnel onto the central parade grounds and then made our way up onto the fort's ramparts.

"I hope we don't run across no moccasins," Kyle whispered as we stepped over the chain and past the danger sign.

"The moccasins have probably all gone to bed," I assured him, though I doubted that was true. It still surprised me that someone like Kyle would be so scared of snakes.

After reaching the southeast bastion we climbed down the crumbling stairs into the sand-filled chamber and flicked on our flashlights. Immediately I saw something dark and quick dart into a hole in the brick. I couldn't hold back a yelp of disgust.

"What is it?" Kyle asked. "What'd you see?"

"A rat."

"You're not afraid of rats, are you?"

"No," I said. "I just don't like them very much."

"Don't worry. They won't bother us. They'll stay hidden as long as we're down here."

"I know," I said, but I half-expected one to jump out and sink its slimy yellow teeth into my throat.

We walked across the sand a few steps and propped up our flashlights so that their beams gave us some light.

"About here, wasn't it?" Kyle asked.

"I think so."

He spit into his hands and seized a shovel. "Well, let's find us some more gold!"

I plunged my own shovel into the sand and quickly buried all thoughts of rats. Kyle dug alongside me and soon it was like we were in a race. I was glad to be able to pour my energy and anger into the work and I didn't let up even when my lower back began to ache. Not that it was fast work. We had to let each shovelful of sand fall slowly from the blade so we could see if anything was in it. Still, both Kyle and I pressed on, sifting through the sand like star-nosed moles looking for worms.

After about fifteen minutes, however, I noticed Kyle digging into a pile of sand to my left.

"Hey, I already looked through there."

Kyle stopped and studied the sand around him. "You sure?"

"Yeah. I think so, anyway."

"Well, he-ell."

I leaned on my shovel handle. Kyle lit up a cigarette and handed me one. I didn't inhale so deeply this time.

"You know," I said, blowing out some smoke, "we need to get more systematic."

Kyle nodded. "Yeah. We're wastin' time this way."

"Maybe we could stake out the sand into square sections, say ten feet on a side? Once we're done with one area, we can move onto the next."

"Good idea," Kyle said, taking another puff. "We gotta get somethin' to run the sand through too. Some sort of a sifter."

"Does Ray have anything like that?"

"Don't think so. We could rig somethin' up, though. I saw some wire screening that might work."

"And maybe bring some buckets too."

"Yeah."

When we finished our cigarettes we decided to dig a little more. I still expected to hit the mother lode, but all we found were some rusty nails and pieces of wood. After half an hour, frustrated and worn-out, we decided to call it a night.

"Maybe there ain't no more gold in here," Kyle said, his voice edged with disappointment.

"Maybe," I said. "But we can't know that until we give it a complete look. We'll just have to come back tomorrow and tackle it differently."

"Yeah. You're right."

We buried the shovels over against the wall of the brick chamber. Then we sneaked back out through the bastion window, careful to replace the two-by-fours behind us.

Chapter 12

We walked to the lab's tool shop as soon as we'd finished breakfast the next morning. Kyle pulled out a roll of wire mesh that looked like it would be just right for sifting out anything bigger than a dime.

"I'll get goin' on a frame," Kyle told me. "You cut out a square of that wire."

"How big?" I asked, picking up some wire snips. "About a yard on each side?"

"Maybe a little smaller. Say, two feet. No, two and a half. Leave some around the edges so we can trim it off after we nail it onto the frame."

While I cut out the wire mesh Kyle found a one-by-two board and used the shop circular saw to cut out four pieces of wood with 45-degree bevels on each end. He nailed the four pieces into a square, and then I attached the wire with some heavy-duty staples. After trimming off the extra wire, we had ourselves a sand sifter.

"Ain't much to look at, but it'll do the job," Kyle said.

"I was thinking we ought to take a lantern," I said. "We're going to burn through those flashlight batteries in a hurry."

"We've got a Coleman gas lamp. I'll bring it along tonight."

I leaned against the bench that held the circular saw. "I wish we could go over there right now."

"Yeah. Too risky, though. Want to go down to the village? We could get us some more coin rolls."

"Good idea. It's almost tamale time too."

Kyle grinned. "Yeah. Tamale time. I can dig that."

We pedaled the two miles to the village. After shooting the breeze with Mr. D for a few minutes, we each bought a tamale and an Icee, then sat down on the curb outside the store to enjoy our snack. A steady line of cars—probably from Mobile—drove over the bridge pulling Boston Whalers or other smaller boats on trailers. A number of larger boats sailed or motored in and out of the main marina across the road.

"I wonder why it's so busy today," I said.

"Friday."

"Oh yeah. I forgot." The past week had flown by, and at this rate it wouldn't be too long before I'd be getting ready to fly back to California. Even after the fight with my dad, the thought sat heavily in my stomach. "You and your folks going to stay on after the classes finish up?" I asked.

Kyle shrugged. "Don't know. If they offer Ray a permanent job at the lab, he might stay. Mom and Annie and me'll prob'ly go on back to Birmingham—or maybe Mobile, where my aunt and cousins are."

"Why do you move around so much, anyway?"

He took another bite of tamale. "I kinda wondered that myself when I was younger," he said. "The way I figure it, Ray's a good guy and a hard worker, but he don't like a lotta bull, know what I mean?"

"Not really."

"When Ray thinks his boss ain't doin' somethin' right or ain't treatin' him with enough respect, he don't put up with it."

"What's wrong with that?"

Kyle wadded up his tamale wrapper and tossed it in the trash can. "Well, nothin', if you don't mind gettin' fired. Thing is, for most jobs, you gotta kiss a little backside now and then. Ray don't know how to do that. Someone gives him crap, he gives it right back. Before ya know it, he's lookin' for a new job."

"Bummer."

"You got that right. Especially for my mom and Annie. I like Ray, but I wish he could get along with folks better."

I wondered if Kyle had ever blown up at Ray like I had at my dad the night before. But before I had time to dwell on it I spotted several guys walking over from the marina. Even from a distance I recognized their blue caps. "Hey, aren't those the guys from the salvage boat?"

Kyle nodded. "Yep. Not the same ones as before, but they got the same hats."

"I'm going to talk to them," I said, standing up.

Kyle smiled and shook his head. "They ain't gonna let you onto that boat, Mike."

"I know that. But we might find out what they're looking for."

We intercepted the three men as they reached the Bait 'n Stuff parking lot. "Excuse me," I said, stepping in front of them. I quickly realized they weren't like the hired hands I'd seen before. Their faces carried an air of authority about them.

"Do you work on the *Reef Wrecker*?" I asked, surprised at the confidence in my voice.

The man in the middle returned my gaze. "That's right, son. I'm the captain."

He looked like a captain too, with curly salt-and-pepper hair and beard and deep crow's-feet chiseled around his brown eyes.

"What can I do for you?" he asked, squinting at me as if he were sighting across a sun-splashed sea surface.

"Well...sir," I began, remembering to adopt the Southern formalities. "I'm a coin collector, and I heard you're looking for gold coins on that wreck."

The captain glanced at the men with him and chuckled. "I guess it's no secret, is it? Yes, son, we sure wouldn't mind finding some gold."

"I don't mean to be nosy, but I was wondering if the coins you're looking for are American or Spanish or what?"

The captain chewed his bottom lip, studying me closely. "Well, I guess I can tell you," the captain said with a cool smile, "if you promise not to spread it around. We hope to find a few gold coins from the New Orleans Mint."

"Do you think they'd be valuable to...you know...to collectors? Or are you just interested in their bullion value?"

The captain seemed more relaxed now. "Well, we're always interested in what will bring the most profit, of course. A few rarities would help us offset the high cost of a venture like this."

"Thank you, sir," I said.

"My pleasure."

As they started to go, I said, "Excuse me, but could I ask just one more question?"

"Go on," the captain told his two companions. "I'll see you inside." Then he turned to Kyle and me. "Yes?"

"Well, I was reading through my coin book and I saw that the Confederate States minted a few silver half dollars with their own design on them. Um, do you think there's a chance you'll find anything like that? Maybe in gold?"

The man's face stiffened and his brown eyes narrowed. "No," he said flatly. "Did someone tell you that?"

My confidence evaporated. "N-no sir. I just thought...I mean, it just seemed like there might..."

"What he means," Kyle said, "is we thought it'd be cool if the Confederates had made their own money."

"As a matter of fact," the captain said, "the Confederacy did print millions of dollars of paper currency. But to my knowledge, they never minted their own gold coins."

The man stopped and stared straight into my eyes. "Why do you ask? Do you boys know something?"

I could see in the man's intense stare that he, unlike the coin store owner, was deadly serious.

I suddenly needed a bathroom *bad*, but I managed to stutter, "N-no sir. We were just curious."

The man's eyes shifted slowly from me to Kyle and back again. He nodded slightly. "Very good. You boys enjoy the day."

"Yes sir," I croaked as he walked away.

Chapter 13

I am such an idiot!" Kyle and I were pedaling back toward SCUM-Lab, each balancing an Icee in one hand and gripping a handlebar with the other. I couldn't believe what I'd just said to the captain.

"We-ell…"

I could tell by the look on Kyle's face that he didn't disagree. "Do you think he knows we're on to something?" I asked.

Kyle took a sip from his drink. "Doubt it. Then again, we gotta watch what we say from now on. You surprised me, pushin' him hard as you did."

"Yeah. Why didn't I keep my mouth shut?"

"On the other hand," Kyle said, "we got more from him than he got from us."

I glanced over at him. "What do you mean?"

"You saw his face when you asked about Confederates makin' gold coins. If we had any doubt about what they're really lookin' for, that cinched it."

"Yeah…I guess that's right." I'd been so busy worrying

about what I might have given away, I'd forgotten to focus on what we'd learned.

"'Sides," Kyle continued. "What can they do? They don't know squat about what we know or don't know."

"Maybe you're right," I said. "We didn't really give them any reason to think we'd found anything."

"No. If we stay away from 'em and keep cool, we'll be flowin' smoother'n Jack Daniels."

* * *

That night we returned to the fort armed with our new sand sifter, two buckets, Kyle's Coleman lantern, and some wooden stakes to mark out our grids. We began by working over the same area we'd started the night before, but this time we kept track of exactly what we did. I paced out a ten-foot square and marked it with wooden stakes. Kyle turned the buckets upside down to act as a raised base for the sifter. Then we retrieved the buried shovels and got to work.

We worked side by side, searching one shovelful of sand at a time. Right away I was glad we'd made the sifter. Now instead of slowly shaking the sand from the shovel blade we could just dump it through the screen. If anything was in the sand, the screen caught it. Of course, we had to move the buckets and the sifter every couple of minutes as the sand piled up underneath it, but that was no problem. After half an hour we'd managed to dig down three feet in our ten-by-ten grid.

"How far down you figure we oughta go?" Kyle said as we paused to assess our progress.

"I was wondering the same thing. How deep do you think the sand is in here?"

Kyle studied the chamber. "Six, maybe eight feet."

"That's what I was guessing too. You think we need to dig all the way to the bottom?"

"Wouldn't think so. We found the first one up near the top, right?"

"Yeah. Though the more I think about it, the stranger that is."

Kyle scratched the whiskers on the side of his face. "Know what you mean. If the gold's been in the fort since the Civil War, but all the sand washed in a long time *after* the Civil War, how'd that double eagle get up near sand surface? It don't make sense."

"No," I agreed. "It doesn't."

"Fact is, we don't know how that coin got in here. We're just takin' a wild guess there's more."

"Yeah," I said. "But especially after talking to that captain today, I've got a feeling there is."

"Me too. All we gotta do is keep lookin'."

We decided that three feet was probably deep enough for our excavations, at least for the first round. If we didn't find anything in that layer, then we could always come back and dig deeper. I paced off a new ten-foot grid and we got back to work.

As it became clear that we weren't going to make a quick score, our initial excitement leveled off. Soon we fell into a steady rhythm of digging, lifting, and sifting. We didn't find any gold, but we uncovered all kinds of "priceless artifacts," from bailing wire and bottle caps to half a dozen beer cans from the early 1960s. We used the sand from each new grid to fill in the hole from the previous grid. Every ten or fifteen minutes we paused to take a break.

As we started in on our fifth grid, however, a brick from above suddenly struck the sand next to me. "Crap!" I said, belatedly leaping to one side. I stared up at the ceiling to see if more were on their way.

Kyle picked up the brick. "This woulda dented your skull," he observed.

"Yeah. Maybe we should be wearing hard hats." I said it as a joke, but realized it wasn't such a bad idea. "You think this whole place could collapse in on us?" I asked, peering up at the ancient conglomeration of brick and decaying mortar overhead.

Kyle wiped his hair from his eyes and looked up. "Doubt it. The fort's been here what, a hundred years? What're the chances it's gonna come down this week?"

"Pretty small, I guess. Still, maybe we should call it a night and come back tomorrow."

"I can live with that," said Kyle.

* * *

The next morning Kyle and I took Annie fishing down at the beach—or rather, *she* took *us* fishing. She scored a couple of nice white trout while we both struck out. We were heading back to Kyle's place when we spotted Dr. Halsted's wife Becky outside of the lab's main office. She was talking to a man wearing a dark blue cap.

"Ain't that the captain of the *Reef Wrecker*?" Kyle asked.

"Yeah, looks like it," I said. "Come on."

Instinctively we ducked behind the corner of the gymnasium and pulled Annie in beside us.

"Why are we waitin' here?" she complained.

"Shhh!" Kyle said. Then to me he whispered, "Whadda ya think he's doin' here?"

Becky and the captain stood about fifty yards from us, turned away so we couldn't hear what they were saying. "I don't know," I told Kyle. "Maybe it has something to with yesterday."

"What happened yesterday?" Annie asked.

"None of your business," Kyle hissed, trying to keep his voice down. "I'll bet you're right, Mike."

Becky and the captain talked for about a minute. Then the captain walked over to a dark green Thunderbird, started it up, and drove out through the laboratory gates.

After the car had turned left toward the village, Kyle said, "Let's go see what he wanted."

We intercepted Becky as she was walking toward the mess hall.

"Mornin', Mrs. Halsted," Kyle said.

I suppressed a grin. Kyle, of course, could have called her Becky by now, but I was pretty sure he used the "Mrs."

as a reminder that she was still married—even if she didn't act like it.

Becky turned toward us. "Well, boys. What a coincidence." She spoke slowly and ran her fingers lazily through her black ponytail, like a cat grooming its fur.

"W-why's that?" I sputtered. I didn't like Becky, but that didn't stop the wave of desire that suddenly surged through me. Certain women, I'd recently discovered, emitted clouds of pheromones that drove males crazy. Becky was one of them. She knew it too.

"Well," she purred, "a man just came by askin' about y'all."

Kyle feigned surprise. "Is that so? What'd he want with us?"

Becky's mouth turned up in a knowing smile, as if she was looking straight through our put-on ignorance. "He said there were some boys down at the village askin' about gold coins. Thought they might be from here."

"Why'd he think that?" I asked.

"Said it was just a hunch. Plus he saw them pedalin' back this way afterwards."

"Don't sound like anyone I know," Kyle said. "What about you, Mike?"

"Nope."

"But," Annie burst in, "y'all took my bike to the—"

Kyle lightly batted her in the back of the head.

"Ow!"

"Yeah, the day before," Kyle said. "But we don't know what that guy's talkin' about."

"So what'd he want?" I asked.

"Didn't really say," Becky answered in her lazy drawl. "Just said he wanted to talk to 'em, that's all."

"Hmmm," I said, trying to appear calm. Inside my chest, though, my heart was running a sprint—from Becky's sex appeal or the captain's inquiries, I couldn't be sure.

"Don't worry," Becky told us, her knowing grin growing wider and more annoying. "I told him I hadn't seen anyone fittin' that description around here."

I trusted her words about as much as I trusted a scorpion not to sting me.

Chapter 14

For the next week we returned to the fort every night. We tried to go early so we could do our digging and get back to the lab without attracting attention, but our absence didn't pass unnoticed.

"Where've you been?" my dad asked when I returned from our third night of excavating. "We missed you at the volleyball game tonight."

"Kyle and I were just hanging around."

"You go fishing?"

"No. We just walked over to the dock to see if anything was going on."

My dad gave me one of those parental looks—the kind that pleaded for attention. Since we'd had the big fight I'd done what I could to avoid him, and neither of us had brought up what had happened. But it didn't take a genius to see that the fight had jammed things up between us like a blood clot. Now my dad cleared his throat. "Look, son, I've been thinking about what you said last week."

I didn't want to get into it with him again, but knew I

couldn't just leave, so I shifted my gaze to the floor.

"And you're right," my dad said. "I haven't fully appreciated how difficult all of this must have been."

"I hate it."

He nodded. "I do too. And if there was an easier way, I'd—you know, I did look for jobs out on the West Coast."

I lifted my gaze back toward him. I'd never heard him say that before.

"I applied for more than a dozen of them," he continued. "But there were just too many biologists looking for work. Still, that doesn't excuse what I've put you through."

Just hearing this began to loosen the tightness in my chest.

"You know," he went on, "my parents divorced when I was a kid too, and it hurt like hell."

I knew my grandparents were divorced, but I'd never thought about how it had affected my dad.

"And," he said, "I swore I'd never do that to a son of mine. But here I went and did the exact same thing. I'm not proud of it."

I could hear the pain in his voice. "You couldn't help it," I said, feeling the need to come to his defense. "You and Mom are just too different."

He nodded. "I suppose we should have been able to see that from the beginning. But if we'd never gotten married, we wouldn't have had you. I truly don't know what I would have done then. You're the best thing in my life, son. I am so proud of what you do and who you are."

I blinked back a tear. The truth was that I had never really been sure how he felt, but hearing him say it closed a hole in me, at least for the moment.

"What can I do to make things easier for you?" he asked.

I thought about it, then shook my head. "Nothing." Which was absolutely true. Like Kyle's life, mine was just what it was—even if I didn't like some of it.

"You sure?"

I looked back down to my feet, thinking. Finally I said, "Well, ask before you want me to do something. Don't just assume I can or want to do everything you think I should."

My dad nodded. "Fair enough."

"One more thing," I said.

My dad raised his eyebrows.

"Don't get mad at me for skunking you at cribbage."

He laughed. "It's a deal."

* * *

The next evening at dinner I told Kyle I wouldn't be able to go to the fort that night. "I'm sorry," I said. "I need to help my dad with his quizzes."

"No sweat," Kyle said. "You should spend time with your dad. Anyway, one more day ain't gonna make much difference."

"Cool. Thanks."

We made plans to go fishing the next morning, and then I headed back to our apartment with my dad.

The quiz had just twenty short-answer questions, but

my dad was a stickler on grading. One reason his students seemed to love him so much is that he didn't let them skate. He challenged them to do the best they could—not just in putting down the right words, but spelling them correctly too. Words like coelenterate and ichthyoparasite and echiuroid. Of course, that meant that to grade his exams, I had to learn all of the answers as well as his students. But I had to admit I kind of liked grading the tests and felt very superior whenever I could put a red *X* through a wrong answer or misspelled word.

Grading this quiz, I was glad to see that Linda Garcon only missed one answer out of the twenty. I picked up Rod's answer sheet and hoped I'd get to paint the thing in red marks. Unfortunately I couldn't find a single wrong answer on Rod's paper. I went over it twice, looking for spelling mistakes or even sloppy handwriting, but his answers were perfect. I growled.

My dad looked over from his desk. "Anything wrong?"

"Nothing. Rod got a perfect score."

My dad laughed. "You've really got it in for that guy, don't you?"

"What do you mean?"

"You don't think I notice how you glare at him whenever he's around?"

"I do not!"

"Yes you do."

"Well, do *you* like Rod?"

My dad took a drag on his cigarette and squinted as the smoke wafted into his eyes. "He's a smart guy."

"Yeah, but do you think it's right what he's doing?"

"What do you mean?"

"You know, fooling around with Dr. Halsted's wife."

He exhaled. "So you noticed that."

"Who doesn't? Why does Dr. Halsted put up with it?"

My dad stuck his notes into the desk and pulled out the cribbage board. "I don't know, son."

"I mean, they're married, aren't they?"

"Yeah, they are," my dad said, handing me the cards.

"You and Mom didn't act like that when you were married, did you?"

"No. But that doesn't mean we always acted our best, either. Marriage is a complicated thing."

I began shuffling the cards. "Yeah, but having your wife mess around with a student..."

My dad put the pegs in the cribbage board and looked at me, a slightly amused, slightly surprised look on his face. "Since when did you get to be so mature?"

I ignored the question. "Doesn't Dr. Halsted care what's going on?"

My dad set his cigarette in the ashtray. "Oh, he cares, all right. He cares a lot. Maybe he just doesn't know what to do about it."

"Kyle said he should punch Rod out."

My dad grinned. "That's one way of handling it. But you know Becky is a lot younger than Bob. I think he's afraid that if he makes a big stink, it'll drive her away. He's playing it cool, hoping she'll get over it and come back to him."

"That's a stupid plan," I said. "I agree with Kyle. If Becky's acting that way, Dr. Halsted should just kick her out."

"You never know. He might just do that."

I dealt the cards, and we concentrated on the game for a while. After I beat my dad in the first round he shuffled the deck again. "You hear about the tropical storm?" he asked.

"Which one?" I replied, picking up my hand. There'd already been two or three tropical storms in the Gulf since I'd arrived in Alabama.

"I think they're calling it Caroline. They're expecting it to reach hurricane strength in the next couple of days."

"Is it coming this way?" I asked with more interest.

"Probably not, but there's a whole line of tropical depressions heading across the Atlantic from Africa. It looks like we're in for a pretty exciting hurricane season."

* * *

By the seventh night Kyle and I had dug through the entire area of the brick chamber. We'd unearthed old shoes, a dozen beer cans, hundreds of nails, rotted strands of rope, a couple of old bottles, and balls of tinfoil. The closest thing we got to a gold coin was a Richard Nixon campaign button.

When we finished digging through our last grid, we threw our shovels aside in disgust and plunked ourselves down in the wavering glow of the gas lantern.

"This stinks," Kyle said, pulling out a pack of cigarettes. Seeing that it was empty, he balled it up and threw it at the brick wall nearby.

"Yeah," I said, sharing his frustration.

"What now? Dig deeper?"

"Doesn't seem likely we'll find anything. What do you think?"

"Prob'ly not—unless we want to keep addin' to our nail collection. But I don't get it. If there ain't more double eagles in here, how'd that first one get in here?"

"I know," I said, worrying over the same problem. "Even if they're somewhere else in this fort, how'd that one single coin land here? It's not like someone would just toss it down into the sand."

"That's right. But what if someone was bringin' in the whole load and one fell out?"

I brightened. "Yeah!" Then the logic failed. "But you said it yourself. This sand wasn't here a hundred years ago. So that still doesn't explain how a single coin would end up near the surface."

Then I had a thought that was more depressing—one I'd never had in our previous conversations. "Wait a minute."

Kyle looked at me.

"What if," I told him, "the gold *was* in here, but someone got here before us?"

"What're you thinkin', Big Mike?"

"I mean, what if someone already came in here, found

all of the double eagles, and just happened to drop or miss one of them while they were hauling out the loot?"

Kyle studied the chamber around us. "Well," he said. "It couldn't be the guys on the *Reef Wrecker*. If they'd already found the gold, they wouldn't be workin' so hard out there on that boat."

"True," I said. "But it could have been someone before them."

Kyle absently picked up one of the rusty nails we'd found. "Woulda had to have been a while ago. When I first discovered this place it didn't look like nobody'd been here for a long time."

"But it's possible, right?"

Kyle tossed the nail back into the sand. "I s'pose so. Yeah."

We both fell silent, not knowing what to do next. Finally Kyle said, "Well, should we head on back?"

"I guess so."

We both stood, but just as I picked up my shovel, I heard a noise like the scrape of sandpaper. It seemed to be coming from the direction of the stairwell.

I froze and Kyle reached down to extinguish the lantern.

We stood quietly, our senses on full alert. I heard nothing more for a few seconds. Then I thought I heard a couple more rasping sounds, like quick footsteps on sandy brick.

"You hear that?" I whispered.

"Sure did," Kyle said. "Come on."

We plowed through the sand and hurried up the stairs. At the top we stopped and surveyed the ramparts. A warm Gulf breeze washed over our skin, and a gibbous moon lit the fort like a medieval castle. We strained to see any sign of movement.

"I don't see anything. Do you?"

"No," Kyle said.

"What do you think it was? Rats?"

Kyle shook his head. "If it was rats, they had to be big suckers."

I shivered at the thought. "You think it was a person?"

"Sounded like it."

"Come on, let's get out of here."

* * *

Kyle and I went up to my room the next morning after breakfast. "Let me see that coin again," he said.

Ever since we'd found it, I'd been hiding the double eagle in a little slot between two boards on the back of my dresser. I reached behind the dresser now and pulled out the coin in the little plastic sleeve that protected it.

Kyle sat down on my bed and slid the double eagle out. He held it by its rims like I'd taught him and stared at it as if he were trying to will it into revealing some hidden information. The gold piece wasn't talking.

"So," Kyle said. "Let's go over what we know. We got this gold coin that may or may not be real."

I sat down next to him. "Right."

"How it got in that fort's anybody's guess. Might be more in there. Might not."

"Right."

"If there's more, we ain't got the faintest idea where they are."

"Right again. And don't forget," I added, "that someone else might know what we're up to and might be watching what we're doing."

"Mm-hmm. So basically what we're sayin' is we're pretty much outta luck."

"Yeah," I said. "Except that we still have this one coin."

"Which may or may not be real."

I flopped down on my back and listened to the depressing coo of the mourning doves outside my window. We'd hit a snag, but I wasn't ready to give up. "Kyle," I said, "The more I go over it in my mind, the more I believe that double eagle is the real thing. I mean, sure, someone could have minted it as a memento a lot later, but how would they come up with that particular design? And why hasn't anyone ever heard of it?

"And," I continued, propping myself up on my elbow, "if there's one coin like that there's got to be more. The only logical place for the others to be is inside of that fort."

Kyle slipped the double eagle back into its sleeve. "Maybe. But don't you think you might just be wantin' something that ain't true? Even if there was gold inside that fort, don't you think someone woulda taken it out again pretty quick? If not durin' the war, then after?"

Kyle was making perfect sense, but my mind didn't want to believe we'd come to a dead end.

"C'mon," Kyle said. "Let's go down to the village. Instead of dreamin' about phantom coins, let's get us a couple rolls of real ones."

I sighed and stood up. "Okay." I returned the double eagle to its secret hiding place and was starting to put on my sandals when a thought stopped me. "Kyle?"

"What?"

"You remember that old guy we met at the beach, the first time we went fishing together?"

"That weird white-haired guy?" Kyle asked, walking to the door.

"Yeah."

"What about him?"

"Well, you remember we were talking about the treasure hunters and he said he didn't think they'd find any gold?"

"So what?"

"Didn't you think he sounded like he knew something?"

"Sounded like he'd fried his brain in the sun."

I snorted. "Maybe. But I think there was something he wasn't telling us. Before we call it quits, let's go talk to him again. See if he really knows anything or not."

Kyle turned toward me, his hand on the doorknob. "I told ya. Old coots like him are a dime a dozen down here. On the island they call 'em old conchs, like the shells.

They got all kinds of wild stories, but most of 'em ain't nothin' but tall tales."

"Yeah, but what can it hurt to talk to him? Let's find out what he knows. Then we can go down to the village."

Kyle rolled his eyes. "Now I know why you Yankees won the war. You don't never give up."

I grinned at him. "Not when there's gold involved."

Chapter 15

Should we tell him what we've found?" I asked Kyle as we walked along the beach toward the old man's house.

"Are you crazy? Why'd we do that?"

"I didn't say I *wanted* to tell him," I said, cockleshells and clamshells crunching under my feet. "But if we just, you know, hit a point where we have to say something to get more information..."

Kyle picked up a piece of driftwood and tossed it into the surf.

"Do you think he's trustworthy?" I asked.

"I guess," Kyle said. "You know, you get a feelin' about someone who ain't shootin' straight with you. I don't get that from him."

"Me neither."

When we reached the spot even with the old weathered house we turned away from the beach. We followed a path through shallow dunes covered with sea oats and reed grass and emerged at the rear of the house. The man was sitting on a spacious back porch in an old plank-style deck chair, smoking his pipe and reading a newspaper. He didn't seem to notice us until we were almost to the porch steps. I gave a little cough.

The old man put down the newspaper and looked at us blankly through his pale blue, sun-bleached eyes. "Yes?"

"Um, excuse me, sir," I began, wishing I'd paid more attention to the man's name. "I don't know if you remember, but we talked out on the beach there a couple of weeks ago."

Still no sign of recognition.

"We were fishing," I reminded him, "and we talked to you about the treasure hunters offshore."

A light seemed to go on for him. "Oh yes. Now I recall you boys. You are Michael, is that correct?"

"Yes sir," I replied, astounded by his memory.

"And you, sir, are…don't tell me. You are Kyle. Kyle Daniels—the First!" he said triumphantly.

Kyle grinned. "Yes sir."

The man let out a chuckle that turned into a cough. He set down the pipe, took out a handkerchief, and held it over his mouth while the cough subsided. "I've always meant to give up this thing," he said, nodding at the pipe, "but I've never seemed to shake it."

"I have the same problem with cigarettes, Mr., um—"

"Dubois," he said. "Anton Dubois. Come on up, boys, and get out of the sun for a few minutes."

We climbed five warped gray steps that had seen their

last paint many years before. At the top of the porch I turned to see a flawless view of the Gulf of Mexico. The *Reef Wrecker* bobbed in the gentle swells about a mile off-shore.

"Wow," I said. "This is nice."

"As you can see, the house needs some care," Mr. Dubois said, "but I find it agreeable on the whole."

"How long have you lived here?" Kyle asked.

"All my life, more or less. And my father before that. And his mother—my grandmother—before that. My great-granddaddy came here as a squatter and earned a living by running fresh fish to Mobile. When he married my great-grandmother, he built this house for her."

As charmed as I was by the story, I was eager to get to the point. "So," I said, "your family was here during the Civil War?"

"Have a seat, boys," Mr. Dubois said, gesturing to a couple of folding lawn chairs. "I do not have much to offer, but may I serve you some iced tea?"

I was about to say no thanks, but Kyle cut in. "That sounds fine, sir. Can I give ya a hand?"

Mr. Dubois stood and smiled. "Thank you, Mr. Daniels, but even at my age I suppose I can manage some tea."

The moment the man disappeared into the house I whispered to Kyle, "Why did you say yes? We could be here all day!"

Kyle relaxed into his chair. "Mike, you gotta learn some Southern hospitality. Ain't polite to refuse refreshment, especially when we just showed up outta nowhere on his back porch. It's good manners to stay and talk a while."

I slumped down in the other lawn chair, but I couldn't sit still.

"Stop jigglin' your legs," Kyle said. "You're gonna shake the porch apart."

Mr. Dubois emerged five minutes later carrying a tray with three glasses of iced tea and a plate loaded with graham crackers. He again apologized for the meager fare. "I don't receive many visitors these days. My son and daughter live in Atlanta and cannot get away very often."

"Thanks." Kyle selected a graham cracker and took a bite. "This is just what the doctor ordered."

Mr. Dubois' thin, chapped lips cracked into a smile.

I took a big gulp of iced tea and almost choked, realizing that the sugar molecules in the glass outnumbered the tea by three or four to one.

"So, boys," Mr. Dubois said, setting down his glass. "I assume this is more than a social call. When I was your age, I would have preferred fishing or getting into mischief to visiting with an old man whose main activity is watching the world go by."

"No sir," Kyle said. "Fact is, we had some questions we thought you might be able to answer for us."

"I will be happy to make an attempt."

"Well, sir, we was wonderin' if you could tell us more about that ship them guys is salvagin' out there. You said you thought they was lookin' for gold, but you didn't think they'd find it. Why'd you say that?"

Mr. Dubois' eyes flashed for an instant, then he reached for his pipe. "I can see that this might call for more tobacco."

I had to stop my leg from jiggling again as Mr. Dubois slowly filled his pipe from a pouch on the table next to him and then unhurriedly lit up. He took a draw from the pipe, leaned back in his chair, and patiently blew out a thin column of smoke.

"That's better," he said. "Now, the ship you are referring to is the *Skink*, as far as we know."

"Yes sir," Kyle answered. "It was a double-wheeled steamship or somethin' like that."

"That is correct," Mr. Dubois answered. "More importantly, it had a shallow draft that would have allowed it in and out of ports like Mobile Bay. And those boys out there seem to have it on authority that the ship was carrying some gold from New Orleans. So far so good?"

"Yeah," I said. "I mean yes sir. That's what we heard. What do you think happened to the gold?"

Mr. Dubois took another drag on his pipe. "Well, Mr...."

I realized I'd never given the man my last name. "It's Gilbert, but just call me Mike."

"Very well, Mr. Mike Gilbert. To answer that question, we have to explore just when and how the *Skink* sank. For years everyone assumed the ship went down in a tempest more than a hundred miles to the east of here. The ship left New Orleans bound for Havana and simply never reached her destination, so people concluded that she must have foundered during the storm that came through about that time. That would also explain why no one found her remains before now.

"But when historians reexamined the records not long ago," Mr. Dubois continued, "they conjectured that perhaps the ship did not sink in a storm, but was blown apart by a Yankee gunship as it was trying to reach safe harbor somewhere inside Mobile Bay. They discovered records of a ship being sunk trying to run the Union blockade, but they found no proof that it was the *Skink*. Then one of these clever treasure hunters got it in his head that it was the *Skink* that went down, and he organized this salvaging expedition. As you probably know, there have been several articles about all of this in the newspapers over the past year."

I leaned forward in my lawn chair. "But you said you didn't think they'd find gold on the *Skink*. Is that because there wasn't any?"

Mr. Dubois pointed his pipe at me. "Now, no one can say with certainty. But I do believe the *Skink* carried gold. And I believe that those are the *Skink*'s remains. What I do *not* believe is that she was carrying the gold when she went down."

Kyle and I looked at each other, confused. "How could that be?" Kyle asked.

Mr. Dubois stared at us for a long moment as if weighing something in his mind. "You know," he finally said, "over the years I've had any number of historians and treasure hounds come talk to me about all kinds of things.

I could see in their eyes that most of them just wanted to make a quick buck or earn a fast reputation, and I sent 'em packing.

"But," he continued, "I'm getting old now and I'm probably the last one of my line who really cares about the history of this place. I'm wondering, if I show you something, will you treat it with the honor it deserves?"

I didn't have a clue what Mr. Dubois was talking about. Kyle, though, seemed to make a connection with the old man.

"If you think you can trust us, sir, we'll do our best not to let you down."

Mr. Dubois nodded. "Very well. If you'll come with me." He stood up and led us into his house, apologizing again for the mess. "As I said, I do not receive many visitors these days."

I looked around, expecting to see a pigsty, but instead found the old house neat and orderly. A large back room full of antique furniture extended almost the length of the bottom level. Walking on what I guessed were oak hardwood floors, we passed a roomy kitchen with faded yellow wallpaper and appliances that dated back several decades. Finally, near the front of the house, Mr. Dubois motioned us into a smaller room.

"My office."

This was where the neatness ended. Papers, newspapers, photo albums, and books were piled on every available surface. Even the floor.

He flipped on a ceiling fan, sending loose papers

flying. "I keep assuring myself I will assert my authority over this mess, but I never seem to do so."

"Ain't no worse than my room at home," Kyle said.

"Mine either," I added.

Mr. Dubois began searching through a floor-to-ceiling bookcase that was bursting with books stacked two deep on the shelves. Reaching behind the first row on the fourth shelf, he pulled out a thin volume. "My grandmother was a writer," he said. "You are too young to have heard of her, but she actually created a modest living for herself by writing books about the Civil War after my grandfather died. She wrote under a man's name back then, to increase her chances of reaching a wider audience."

"Is that one of her books?" Kyle asked.

"This? Oh no. This," he said, holding up the book, "is far more precious. It is her diary, written"—he paused to study us—"why, written when she was just a tad younger than you gentlemen are now." He held the diary out so we could see it.

I don't know why, but when my hand touched the smooth leather cover a chill shot up my spine—a chill like the one I'd felt when I touched the bricks in the fort's tunnel. Maybe it was the sudden realization that people my age—people a lot like me—really *were* alive in this very spot more than a hundred years before. Or maybe it was the expectation that Kyle and I had suddenly gotten a lot closer to some answers about the double eagle.

Mr. Dubois cleared his throat. "Now, as I mentioned, my grandmother grew up in this house just as I did. In fact, she and her family were right here during the Battle of Mobile Bay and the capture of Fort Henry in 1864."

"But that was later, wasn't it? After the battle of New Orleans?" I was still struggling with the whole Civil War timeline.

"You are correct, sir! But plenty was happening right here on the island all during the war. Fort Henry was in Confederate hands when New Orleans fell, of course, and despite the Union blockade, Mobile remained one of the most important ports for the South. Hundreds of soldiers moved on and off the island and dozens of blockade-runners ran the Union gauntlet to deliver crucial supplies to Southerners and their armies—and to smuggle cotton back out."

"And is that what your grandma wrote about?" Kyle asked.

"She did. Yes sir. She was gifted with keen powers of observation and, even at your age, recorded everything she saw, including"—Mr. Dubois again paused to study us, unable to resist building the suspense—"including what she and her little brother witnessed on the night of April 24, 1862—only a day before Union forces captured the city of New Orleans."

"What did they see?" Kyle blurted out.

Mr. Dubois cleared a stack of newspapers from a desk and set the diary down. Carefully he opened the ancient journal. The yellowed pages had become brittle, and Mr. Dubois turned each one deliberately and slowly.

"Ah, here it is."

Kyle and I moved in closer and read the elaborately penned handwriting for ourselves.

April 24, 1862

Evening last, Papa asked Jarod and me to take a string of red fish over to Fort Henry for the officers' mess. Just after the guards waved us into the encampment outside the fort we heard the unmistakable chuffing of a paddle wheel steamer coming through the inner passage from the west. She showed no running lights, which was not surprising given the Union's barbaric insistence on stopping trade in and out of our ports. What did surprise me was that instead of continuing on to Mobile as is the practice of most other ships, the steamer docked right here at Fort Henry.

Forgetting our fish delivery duties, Jarod and I hurried down toward the dock. There we saw General Buckford meet with the captain of the steamer. We could not discern their conversation, but moments later a chest was carried off the steamer and conveyed into the fort. I desired to stay and continue watching these strange events, but at that moment a soldier confronted us. As he was not one of the guards who knew us, he ordered us away to complete our errand. We complied without protest. I told Jarod that we could return the next morning for a closer look at the steamer since she was unlikely to leave before her crew could rest and they could take on supplies.

Several hours later, however, I was awakened by a thunderous cacophony. I leaped out of my bed, sure that the most tempestuous storm had engulfed us. Mother led me up to the widow's walk, where we found Jarod and Father staring east through Father's spyglass. In the distance, offshore of Fort Morgan, we witnessed a fiery battle from hell. What appeared to be a paddle wheel steamer had been turned into a blazing pyre. It threw so much light on the sea as to illuminate a Union warship nearby. As we watched, the warship's guns belched fire twice more, but there was no need. The paddle wheel was doomed, and we watched her sink ten minutes later. We know not if any of the crew escaped.

"Wow," I said. "Your grandmother could write! You said she was about our age when she wrote this?"

"Indeed," Mr. Dubois said with a smile. "She goes on to confirm that the stricken ship was the very same she had seen docking at Fort Henry earlier that evening. Oddly, she never mentioned the actual name of the vessel, and for years I speculated which ship it could have been."

"Did you think it was the *Skink*?" Kyle asked.

Mr. Dubois shook his head. "It was not until newspaper

articles of the treasure hunters' activities began appearing last year that I reread my grandmother's journal and began putting two and two together."

"Why wouldn't she just give the name of the ship?" I asked.

Mr. Dubois tapped his finger on the open page of the journal. "I can surmise a number of possibilities."

"If carryin' the gold was such a big secret," Kyle suggested, "maybe no one'd want the ship's identity to be known."

"Yes," said Mr. Dubois. "Even in the deepest South, Union spies and sympathizers lurked everywhere."

"But there's one other problem with this story, ain't there?" Kyle said.

Mr. Dubois smiled. "I can guess what you are going to say, Mr. Daniels."

"The location."

"That's right!" I exclaimed. "Your grandmother wrote that the battle occurred off of Fort Morgan. That's at least three or four miles from where the *Reef Wrecker*'s working, isn't it?"

"Yes it is," Mr. Dubois agreed. "But remember, this coast has been hit by at least half a dozen major hurricanes in the past century. I did a little reading and discovered that storms of such magnitude have often moved wrecks large distances. In fact, I remember that when I was a boy one hurricane tossed the hull of an old wreck onto shore with such fury that it demolished one of the houses here on the island."

"But three miles?" I failed to keep the skepticism out of my voice.

"In some cases, yes."

"So," Kyle said, trying to sum everything up. "You're sayin' the *Skink* stops here at Fort Henry for an hour or two, drops off the chest, then leaves that very same night, where she's blown outta the water. Then along comes a hurricane—"

"Or two or three," Mr. Dubois added.

"Right. And over time the storms carry the wreck all the way to this side of the bay, which is where the treasure hunters found her."

"Do you draw different conclusions?" he asked us. "Because if you do, I would most certainly love to hear them."

"Well, I guess it's all possible," I said, "assuming that Union records were wrong about which way the *Skink* was going. I mean, everyone thinks she was entering the bay when she was sunk, and you're saying she was actually leaving, right?"

"Yes sir. I tend to put more stock in my grandmother's eyewitness accounts than in official Union documents from the time."

"But surely the Confederates kept records too," I persisted. "Records that would have shown the truth."

"Not if they was tryin' to hide the delivery," Kyle said.

"And don't forget," Mr. Dubois said. "It's likely the Confederates destroyed most of their records when Union troops overran the fort two years later, in 1864. It's quite possible no accurate accounts of the events survived."

"Shoot," I said. "So we might not ever really know what happened."

"No." Mr. Dubois smiled. "On the other hand, one piece of evidence would clear up a great deal about this mystery."

"What's that?" I asked.

"Actually finding some of the gold those treasure hunters are looking for."

Kyle and I had been caught up in unraveling the events of April 24, 1862, but Mr. Dubois' statement jolted us back to the present. We looked at each other, neither one wanting to speak first. I could see we were both wrestling with whether we ought to tell Mr. Dubois of our discovery.

The old man saved us from having to decide. After observing us fidget for a moment, he laughed. "Do not fret, boys. I always prefer a mystery that stays mysterious to one that is solved. But I would like to impart a word of advice."

"What?" Kyle asked.

"If the *Skink* was carrying gold—and if that gold is somewhere here on the island—there are people who will stop at nothing to get their hands on it. If I were you, I would keep what I know to myself. And if I may be of further service, please do not hesitate to pay me another visit."

Chapter 16

So where's that leave us?" Kyle asked as we set a fast pace back toward the lab.

"I don't know, but if what Mr. Dubois says is true, everything points to the *Skink* unloading its treasure at the fort that night. Which would mean the gold wasn't out *there* like they thought," I said, pointing toward the *Reef Wrecker*. "Instead it was right here on the island."

"Yeah, but that don't mean it stayed here."

"I know," I admitted. "But if someone took it out again, how come we've never heard of it? I mean, Kyle, it's been more than a hundred years! And you're telling me that in all that time not a single piece of that gold would have ever turned up?"

"Another ship could've taken it out and got itself sunk," Kyle suggested.

"Oh, come on! What are the odds of that happening?"

Kyle grinned. "Easy now, Big Mike. I ain't tellin' you

that's what happened. I'm just tryin' to figure all the angles."

I took a deep breath and told myself to relax. I looked at Kyle. "So what do you really think? Is the gold still in the fort?"

"If I had to guess one way or the other, I'd say fifty-fifty—which ain't half bad."

"But why would they bring it here in the first place?" I pressed. "I understand why they'd want to get the gold out of New Orleans, but why send it here?"

A ghost crab scuttled out of the way of our moving feet. "Most likely they didn't know where else to send it," Kyle said. "Mobile was about the last Southern port still open. They probably figured Fort Henry was as safe a place as any to keep it until they knew what to do with it. Then maybe the gold just kind of got lost in the shuffle."

I nodded. "Okay, I can buy that. So that means all we have to do is keep looking?"

"Yes and no," said Kyle. "I mean, we're pretty sure it ain't in that room we been diggin' through. But that still leaves the rest of the fort. Even supposin' they let us look wherever we want—which they won't—how're we gonna find the gold in that huge place?"

I slowed, my brief optimism plunging toward despair.

Kyle cut his stride to match mine. "I ain't sayin' we can't do it. I'm sayin' it's gonna take some time."

"So you want to keep looking?" I halted.

"He-ell yeah. 'Sides," he said, sweeping his hand

toward the rest of the island, "what else we gonna do out here?"

My mood rebounded. "Okay. Good. Where should we start?"

"I been thinkin' 'bout that," Kyle said as we resumed walking. "Maybe we should go ahead and pay admission and see if we can get more info from the signs or the folks who work there. At least we'd be lookin' around in broad daylight when it's easier to see."

"Good idea," I said. "You want to go after lunch?"

He grinned. "I'll have to check my appointment calendar, but yeah. I'm in."

We headed straight to the mess hall and loaded up our trays with blue crab, spinach, corn bread, and pecan pie. I spotted my dad at one of the tables with Dr. Halsted, and they motioned us over to join them.

"Long time no see," my dad quipped as we sat down. "What kind of trouble you two been getting into this morning?"

"Not near enough," Kyle shot back, using his fork to split open a thick blue crab claw.

"We just took a walk on the beach to see if the tide washed up anything interesting," I said.

My dad snorted. "Yeah, right. And I just inherited a million dollars from a long-lost aunt."

"What did you do with your class today?" I asked, changing the subject.

Dr. Halsted answered. "My students went with your old man's class on a joint field trip out to Low-John Island."

Low-John was a sand island off the other end of Shipwreck Island. Kyle and I had seen it on navigation charts hanging in the wet lab and library.

"Why'd y'all go there?" Kyle asked. "Is that where this crab came from?"

"As a matter of fact, it is."

Kyle held up a crab claw. "In that case, thanks. We should've gone with you."

"Dr. Halsted and I thought our classes might benefit by pooling their newfound knowledge," my dad explained. "His phycology class taught my kids about marine algae, and my class taught them what a mistake they'd made studying plants instead of invertebrates."

"Ouch!" Dr. Halsted made a mock grimace as he dipped a crab leg into a saucer of melted butter. "So what do you boys have planned for the afternoon? Going to storm Fort Henry?"

Dr. Halsted said it as a joke, but my hand jerked and a chunk of spinach fell off my fork.

Kyle looked at me with one raised eyebrow. "How'd ya know?" he said, turning to Dr. Halsted and my dad. "I want to show Mike it was just dumb luck the Union forces were able to take that fort and win the war."

My dad and Dr. Halsted laughed and the talk moved on to other subjects. Dr. Halsted asked us if we'd been following the news about the latest hurricane.

"You mean Caroline?" I asked, referring to the storm my dad had mentioned the week before. "I thought that one fizzled."

"It did," Dr. Halsted said. "This one's called Elsa."

"She looks like a real badass too. Might even be worse than Camille," my dad said, referring to the devastating hurricane that had flattened coastal Mississippi several years earlier. Of course, my dad was prone to exaggerate the threat of apocalyptic events, so I didn't take him all that seriously until Dr. Halsted chimed in.

"She's already a Category Two," he said. "They're expecting her to grow even stronger in the next few days. The National Weather Service is saying she could reach a Four or even a Five."

Category Five, of course, was the strongest, most devastating storm possible.

Kyle whistled. "Where's she headed?"

My dad pushed his tray back. "Not sure. Right now they're predicting landfall somewhere between Panama City Beach, Florida, to Tampico, Mexico."

"So the storm could end up anywhere," I said.

"Right," my dad agreed. "She'll probably miss us—if she doesn't peter out before then. Still, don't be surprised if we all have to bail out in a hurry one of these days."

* * *

After lunch I grabbed some cash from my room and Kyle and I walked to Fort Henry. I felt weird going through the main entrance after we'd sneaked in through the bastion so many times. I paid our admission and picked up one of the maps sitting next to the cash register.

"Where do we even begin?" I asked, opening the map to the complicated diagram of the fort.

"You got me," Kyle said, studying the layout over my shoulder.

The fort covered six acres and contained half a dozen buildings. The outer walls stretched almost half a mile around the perimeter and undoubtedly held a dense warren of other rooms and storage areas.

"Y'all want a tour?" the woman at the cash register asked us.

I lowered the map and looked at Kyle. He shrugged.

"Is one starting soon?" I asked.

"We don't have anything scheduled, but I'm sure Dolores would be happy to show you around." She left the room and returned with another woman about my grandmother's age. The woman had stuffed her gray hair under a safari-type hat, and wore an outfit of pink shorts, a blinding white T-shirt with a logo of the fort on it, and equally dazzling white tennis shoes.

"Good afternoon!" she greeted us. "You boys needin' a tour?"

"Yes ma'am," we both answered together.

"If it's not any trouble," Kyle added.

"'Course not! That's what I'm here for. My name's Dolores. And you might be?"

"Mike."

"Kyle."

"Well, it's good to see young people interested in the history of our great nation. Are you ready to begin?"

Dolores launched her tour with a stern lecture on why the Civil War was not, in fact, a *civil* war because that term implies an uprising of citizens to overthrow the government. The South, she said, simply wanted to establish a *separate* government. Therefore the war should be called by its "correct name," the War between the States.

After that little verbal excursion, we all walked—or rather bounced—out of the office. Despite her advanced age, Dolores had more energy than a kangaroo fleeing a crocodile.

The fort, she told us as we followed her up the brick ramp to the east-facing ramparts, was intended to protect the mouth of Mobile Bay, but was ill equipped for the task during the Civil War. "Fort Henry was designed to have more than one hundred cannon facing all sides. But only twenty-six were ever installed."

Kyle and I looked at each other, surprised. "Why was that, ma'am?" he asked.

"Well," Dolores said, "one reason was because the South was severely short of artillery pieces. But another reason was that General Buckford was sure the fort would never be attacked."

"Buckford," I said, remembering what Mr. Dubois' grandmother had written in her diary. "He was in charge of the fort?"

"Not just this fort." Dolores removed her hat and waved it toward Mobile Bay. "He also commanded Fort Morgan and all the other defenses of southern Alabama."

"Wasn't he worried the Union would take the fort?"

Kyle asked. "It'd be tough to defend with only a few guns."

"That involves some interesting speculation," Dolores answered, obviously pleased by our curiosity. "Accordin' to accounts of the time, Commander Buckford might have been lookin' out for his own interests as well as those of the Confederacy."

"What do you mean?" I asked.

Dolores put her hat back on. "Apparently it was common knowledge that the good general was getting a cut of all the cargo goin' in and out of Mobile Bay with the blockade-runners. But most of the runners entered and exited the bay through the channel that runs right by Fort Morgan. So," she asked us with a gleam in her eye, "which fort do you suppose had more cannon, Fort Morgan or Fort Henry?"

I went ahead and stated the obvious. "Fort Morgan."

"You got it, honey. Old General Buckford—bless his heart—wanted to make sure he kept those Union warships as far offshore as possible so he'd get his piece of the pie. But unfortunately he never got a chance to enjoy whatever riches he gained. After the fall of Fort Henry and Fort Morgan, the general was taken prisoner and, like so many soldiers on both sides, he died of dysentery."

"Wow."

"But back to the main point," Dolores continued. "Having all the firepower on that side of the bay left this side wide open for an attack. The real reason Mobile kept operating as long as it did was not because it was the best-defended harbor in the Confederacy. It was because the generals in Washington kept ordering Farragut, the Union naval commander, to deploy his ships on other assignments—missions that were generally unsuccessful. If Farragut had been allowed to attack Mobile when he wanted to—in 1862—the port would have been shut down and the entire war might have ended earlier."

A pleasant breeze was blowing in from the bay and across the ramparts where we were standing. Dolores paused and took a deep breath. "I never get tired of that salt air." Then she turned back to us. "Do y'all have any more questions?"

"I have one," I said. "The Union captured the fort in 1864, right?"

"Correct."

"Well, did you ever hear of Commander Buckford or anyone else hiding anything so the Union forces wouldn't find it?"

"Like weapons and equipment? As a matter of fact, Southern forces often destroyed their positions so they wouldn't be useful to the enemy. Right across the water there," she said, pointing to the mainland side of the Intracoastal Waterway, "the Rebels blew up Fort Powell so it wouldn't fall into Union hands."

"Actually I was thinking more about important documents," I said, choosing my words carefully. "Or maybe money."

Dolores smiled. "Oh yes. I'm sure that happened too. But believe me, honey, in the past hundred years, people have gone over this fort with a fine-toothed comb. Not only did the military make extensive modifications to it during later wars, but many historians and archaeologists have also visited the site. If there were any hiding places, someone would have found them by now.

"Now if you'd like to follow me this way," she continued, "I'll show you one of the fort's five bastions." She led us to the top of the northwest bastion—the one we usually sneaked into—and then took us down the circular stairway into its heart. She explained how the bastion jutted out from the main fort so cannons and rifles could protect the fort's outer walls. She described the powder room and showed us how the bastion was cleverly designed to catch rainwater that drained down into a cistern below the center of the floor.

"Just last year, in fact, a local historian crawled around inside the cisterns, and they still appeared to be fully functional. Come this way," she said, hurrying us along. "Before we end the tour, you must see where they installed the disappearing cannon in 1898."

We listened as politely as we could while she proudly described the remaining highlights of the tour. When we reached the iron chain with the sign that read DANGER: CLOSED AREA, she stopped. "Unfortunately, boys, this is as far as we can go."

Even though Kyle and I had crossed the chain many times, I played dumb. "Oh? How come?"

Kyle suppressed a grin.

"Well," said Dolores, "as you'll observe, this part of the

fort is the closest to the ocean. The hurricanes of 1906 and 1916 inflicted considerable damage to the south wall and southeast bastion, and even Camille's storm surge in 1969 severely eroded the fort's foundation. The Southern Sons Society hopes to raise money to stabilize this section of the fort, but because of the cost it likely won't happen for many years."

We thanked Dolores and watched her bounce back along the ramparts toward the fort office. Then we began our own explorations. I especially wanted another look at the officers' quarters, while Kyle thought the ten-hole latrine might offer some hiding possibilities. After another hour of snooping, however, it became obvious that we were getting nowhere, so we decided to give up and head back to the lab. We had just exited the tunnel leading from the latrine and were heading for the exit when we almost collided with a man walking in the other direction.

"Excuse me," I muttered, stepping back.

"What a pleasant coincidence," the captain of the *Reef Wrecker* told us. "I've been looking for you boys."

I felt like bolting, but forced my feet to stay planted.

"That so?" Kyle asked, his voice cool.

"It is," the man replied. "I wanted to ask you a few questions."

"Doubt we'll be able to help you," Kyle said. I was glad he was doing the talking. My throat felt as dry as crumbled brick.

A forced smile crossed the captain's lips. "I wouldn't

be so sure of that. When we met before, you boys asked me about Confederate gold."

"Did we? Can't say as I remember."

"Oh, I think you do," said the captain. "In fact, your friend here distinctly asked about coins that may have been minted by the Confederacy with their own designs."

"What about it?" I rasped.

"Well, I got the feeling you boys might know more than you're letting on. I thought it might be in all our interests if we shared information. Sort of pooled our knowledge."

"Why?" Kyle asked. "Ain't you findin' anything out on that wreck?"

The captain's jaws seemed to clench. "Well, let's just say we'd like it to go a little faster. And with a hurricane possibly heading this way, we're anxious to make as much progress as possible. So what do you say? You boys willing to play ball?"

"We don't know anything," I blurted out.

The captain's nostrils flared. "Is that so? Then what are you doing poking around in this fort?"

"We've just been wantin' to see it," Kyle answered. "What are *you* doin' here?"

All traces of friendliness vanished from the captain's face, and he lowered his voice. "Listen, I've spent ten years of my life looking for the gold the *Skink* was carrying. If you know something about it, you damned well better tell me. If not, you could find yourselves in big trouble."

If the captain thought he could scare Kyle, he didn't know him very well.

"Yeah?" Kyle said, his fists clenching. "Well, that can cut both ways. You don't scare us none, right, Mike?"

"Th-that's right."

"We already told you, we don't know nothin'. Pushin' us around ain't gonna change that. I've dealt with bullies a lot tougher and meaner than you, but if you wanna try somethin', now's your chance."

After our encounter with the rednecks my first week on the island, Kyle had said he would have run away if they'd called his bluff. Now I knew that wasn't true. If the captain tried anything, I had no doubt he was going to meet up with a wildcat. The captain must have sensed it too. He changed tactics.

"You boys know it's a federal crime to remove anything from a historic site?"

"Is that right?" I said, encouraged by Kyle's boldness. "And you're telling us you've declared every treasure you ever found on a shipwreck?"

The captain's face ripened from red to dark purple.

"Besides," I continued, "we haven't found a thing here or anywhere else."

"That's right," Kyle said. "You stay outta our business, we'll stay outta yours."

"You haven't heard the last of this," the captain promised and stormed toward the fort exit.

Chapter 17

Well, so much for working in secret," I muttered. They were the first words either of us had spoken since leaving the fort.

"That guy's full of bull." Kyle's fists were still clenched, and I could hear the adrenaline in his voice.

"But he was poking around the fort himself," I said. "Why would he do that if he didn't suspect something? Maybe he was even the one spying on us the other night."

"Maybe. But what's he gonna do?"

"I can imagine a few things. He looked pretty serious. You don't think he could have found out about our coin, do you?"

"Naw," Kyle said, finally taking a deep breath. "You and me are the only ones who know about it. Well, and maybe old Mr. Dubois, but I don't think he'd tell anyone."

"Right," I said, but I couldn't help wondering if the coin was safe where I'd hidden it in my room.

We crawled through the barbed-wire fence separating the fort from the lab.

"Well," Kyle said, "it don't really matter much now. You heard what the guide said. That fort's been picked cleaner than a dead fish by crabs."

"True," I said. "But remember, we *did* find that coin. And if we found one, there could be others. Didn't you see any place on the tour that might be a good hiding spot?"

"Sure. The whole danged fort."

"Big help."

We reached the back of the barracks and stood in the shade, careful to avoid the fire ant mounds that pocked the sand.

"I mean it," Kyle said. "They coulda hid that gold anywhere."

I sighed. As much as I hated to admit it, I was again feeling doubts about our search. "Yeah. That's what I think too. But still, I'd like to try one more time. Let's go back to the same place and dig all the way to the bottom of that sand."

Kyle shot me a glance, eyebrows arched.

"This'll be the last time," I told him. "I promise."

He relented. "Okay. Guess it's worth a try. You wanna go tonight?"

"We'd better. With that captain snooping around, we may not get too many more chances."

* * *

I climbed the back fire escape to the second floor of the barracks. Since my dad and I had talked a few nights before, he'd been going out of his way to wait for me to go to dinner. His class still kept him busy most other times, but I appreciated that he was making more of an effort. This evening, though, I found the apartment empty, so I went on over to the mess hall.

I didn't find my dad there, either, but just as I left the cafeteria line I saw Linda beckoning me to join her.

"Hi, Mike," she said. "I haven't seen much of you lately. What've you been up to?"

I was pleased she'd noticed my absence. "Kyle and I have been hanging out a lot."

She hooked her brown, sun-streaked hair back behind her ear. "I imagine this island's a pretty fun place to explore," she said, her smile rendering me almost breathless.

"Yeah, it's okay," I said, not daring to reveal how interesting it had actually become.

For the next few minutes I told her about fishing and taking the tour of the fort. She told me how her classes with my dad were going and what she planned to do the coming year. After finishing the last bite of her meal, she wiped her mouth and said, "We've missed you at the volleyball games. Why don't you come tonight?"

I wanted to just yell, *Yes! Yes! Anything to be with you!* Instead I replied, "I'll try, but I've got to do something first."

"Don't take too long. We need someone who really knows how to play out there."

I bussed my dinner tray and hurried back to our apartment. My dad still hadn't shown up, but Kyle knocked on the door a few moments later. He'd had dinner at his house with Annie and his folks.

"You ready?" he asked.

"Yeah. Let's go."

We trotted down the back fire escape and walked to the barbed-wire fence. I was about to climb through when Kyle put his hand on my shoulder. "Hold up."

I followed the direction of his stare and saw a car parked over near the front entrance to the fort. The words "Mobile County Security" had been clearly stenciled onto the side door.

"Son of a barkin' dog," Kyle muttered under his breath.

"What do you make of that?"

"Don't know, but I'll bet it's got somethin' to do with our friend the captain."

"You think so?"

"If I had to put two and two together."

"You think they've put a guard inside the fort?"

"Yeah, or stationed one on the outside. Either way, we're skewered."

"We could get around him," I suggested.

"Maybe. But we got no idea where he's gonna go or where he's gonna look."

As he said this a uniformed man appeared around the corner of the far northwest bastion—the one we'd been sneaking through. A black nightstick and a holstered gun hung from the man's wide leather belt.

Kyle and I quietly retreated before he saw us, but we

continued to watch him from the shadows of the barracks.

"Maybe he'll leave," I whispered.

"Maybe."

When the man reached his car, though, he walked right past it to the front gate. He pulled out a set of keys and flipped through them.

"Man, he's huge!" I said.

"Got that right. Wouldn't want to mess with him."

The man inserted a key in the lock and let himself into the fort, closing the gate behind him.

"Crap," I said. "Now what do you want to do?"

Kyle scratched his cheek. "Ain't much we can do, is there?"

I thought for a moment and shook my head. "I guess not. But," I said, trying to salvage a silver lining, "Linda said she'd be at the volleyball game. You want to go play?"

Kyle disappointment turned into a grin. "Sure."

As we walked toward the pool and volleyball court, the orange sun was sinking into a layer of clouds just above the horizon. Even though it was only the last week of July, the days had begun to grow slightly shorter—another reminder that it wouldn't be too many more weeks before I'd have to leave my dad and this place and go back home to California.

Before I could dwell on that depressing thought, however, we reached the volleyball court. It was empty.

"Linda said everyone would be here," I said, mystified.

"Maybe somethin' came up."

"Like what?" I couldn't imagine what could come up so suddenly.

Kyle lit a cigarette and offered me one. I turned it down. After smoking for a couple of weeks, I'd returned to my original conclusion that smoking was a dumb thing to do. Instead I debated our next move.

"Well, we've still got some daylight left," I finally said. "Let's go talk to Mr. Dubois."

"Again?" Kyle asked. "We were just there."

My suggestion surprised even me. "The old guy has grown on me," I told Kyle. What I didn't say was that since our tour of the fort something had begun to nibble at my brain. I didn't know what it was exactly, but I just felt like Mr. Dubois had more to tell us. "You got any better ideas?"

Kyle shrugged and dropped his cigarette into the sand. "Naw. Let's go."

We set off down the beach and stopped when we got to the old house. Mr. Dubois wasn't on the back porch, but he answered the door when we knocked.

"Another visit so soon?" Mr. Dubois said. "This island cannot be that dull. Or, dare I hope that you have more information about your treasure quest?"

I looked over at Kyle. "We might as well tell him," I said.

"Your call, Big Mike."

"Can we come in?" I asked.

"Of course!" Mr. Dubois said, stepping aside. "I am forgetting my manners."

We all sat down in the back room, looking out at the setting sun. Mr. Dubois again offered us tea, but even Kyle declined. Instead we launched into the complete story of what we'd found—and what we hadn't. It took us about twenty minutes to explain all of our theories and thoughts and dead ends. When we finished Mr. Dubois didn't even light up his pipe. Instead a wide smile slowly spread across his face.

"Boys, let me congratulate you. There have always been rumors of treasure on this island, mostly pirate treasure, and I have to admit I spent a fair portion of my youth searching for it. Now you have fulfilled every young boy's dream."

"But," Kyle said, "that's just it. We got the one coin, but we ain't found the chest."

I joined in. "We don't even know if we should keep looking, and if we do, *where* we should look."

Mr. Dubois finally reached for his pipe and leaned back in his leather chair. "I see your dilemma."

"Do you have any ideas?"

He lit the pipe and seemed to search the cloud of smoke for answers. "I cannot tell you *where* to look," he said. "I probably have less of an idea than you about that. As to whether you should keep looking...well, there I may be able to offer some advice."

"How's that?" Kyle asked him.

"In your tour of the fort," he said, "a promising point leaped out. The part about Commander Buckford."

"Right. The tour guide told us he might not have been on the up-and-up."

"Yeah," Kyle said. "Buckford was supposedly takin' bribes...or a cut of the blockade-runners' profits."

"Don't misunderstand," said Mr. Dubois. "The general was a brave and fine leader, but I must once again defer to my grandmother."

"The diary?" I asked.

Mr. Dubois shook his head. "Excuse me for a moment."

He stood slowly and shuffled out of the room. When he returned he was wearing reading glasses and holding a hardbound book in his hands.

"As I told you before," he said, "my grandmother was an author of some local repute. This is one of her works, *Voices of the Troops*. As Confederate veterans began dying of old age around the turn of the last century, she tracked them down and interviewed those she could locate around here."

He flipped through the pages and stopped.

"Yes, here's an example," he said. "This soldier complains about the officers living in grand fashion while the enlisted men barely had enough to eat. He especially harps on the amount of luxury goods—liquor, mostly—that had been smuggled in aboard the blockade-runners."

He continued to thumb through the book. He read us parts of another interview with a soldier who complained about how undermanned Fort Henry was compared to Fort

Morgan across the bay. The soldier mentioned rumors of corruption among some of the officers, including General Buckford.

"So it appears," Mr. Dubois said, closing the book, "that our commander may not have been as saintly as posterity surmised."

"So you think he kept the gold?" I asked.

"I would wager a fair amount that he did indeed."

"Maybe he spent it," Kyle said. "That could be how he bought the liquor and other stuff."

"It's possible," Mr. Dubois conceded, "but I believe that spending missing Confederate gold may have been too blatant an act, even for a man who appeared to control much of the local economy. If he did receive even minor kickbacks on the blockade-runners' cargo, he would've had plenty of other cash on hand."

"Really?" I asked.

"Certainly. Running the blockade proved so lucrative that a single load of cargo earned enough money to pay for the construction of the blockade-runner itself *and* give the ship's owners a fair profit in the bargain."

Kyle whistled. "Geez."

"That is why so many people flocked to the business. Except for a small few, the ships weren't owned by Confederate patriots. Most of the blockade-runners were built and operated by British businessmen who were out to make a fortune."

Mr. Dubois chuckled, warming to the subject. "Why, in some cases, these fellas would smuggle cotton out of

Southern ports and sell it to the Yankees up in Boston or Philadelphia."

"You're kidding."

"Not at all. One thing I've learned is that while politicians often go to war in the name of God and country, if you dig a little deeper you can usually uncover a much uglier, less noble motive behind the decision. And while the politicians and businessmen earn enormous profits, it is young boys like you who must offer the ultimate sacrifice. That's why I am against wars. Every single one of them."

Those words were about the last thing I expected to hear from Mr. Dubois.

"However, I did not mean to give you two a lecture," Mr. Dubois continued, settling back in his chair. "Returning to our original subject, you asked if the gold might still be in that fort? My answer is yes. Commander Buckford undoubtedly kept it there after he received it. And, in my mind, he undoubtedly hid it when the Union captured the fort."

"But wouldn't someone have gone back to get it?" Kyle asked. "I mean, the woman at the fort told us the general died durin' the war, but surely someone who knew about the gold would've survived."

Mr. Dubois took another puff on his pipe. "My guess would be that anyone who knew about the gold also died in the war. More important, if I had been General Buckford, I would have made sure that as few people as possible knew exactly what was in that trunk or where it was hidden."

"Hmm," I murmured, staring down at my feet. The old man's words had renewed my hope that the gold was still hidden inside of Fort Henry. Unfortunately they had shed no light on exactly where the hiding place might be. I looked back up at Mr. Dubois. "Where would *you* hide the gold if you commanded that fort?"

Mr. Dubois frowned. "I'm afraid I'm not nearly clever enough to address that question. But I imagine it would be a place where no one would think of looking for anything valuable."

"I was thinkin' about the latrines earlier," Kyle said. "Lady at the fort said there was nine different ones in various places."

Mr. Dubois pointed his pipe directly at Kyle. "That, sir, is the kind of thinking I expect the general was doing. I do foresee some problems with that particular possibility, however. For one, enlisted men had to muck out most of the latrines every single day. For another, an officer of the general's stature might have had a certain…let's say *aversion* to having to retrieve his treasure from a 'honey pot'."

Kyle and I both laughed. "You're prob'ly right," Kyle muttered.

"Well, where else could it be?" I asked.

We fell silent for a moment and you could almost hear the gears grinding inside our heads. Suddenly Kyle slapped his knee. "Of course!" he shouted. "We walked over it a hundred times."

"What?" I asked impatiently. "What did we walk over?"

He looked at me. "The cistern!"

"But Dolores said a historian had explored the cisterns recently," I objected.

"Sure, the bastions that are *empty*," Kyle said. "But you think that guy bothered to dig his way through six feet of sand?"

As soon as he said it, I couldn't believe how stupid I'd been. "Oh man, that is so obvious."

Mr. Dubois was grinning. "I think you just may have struck upon something, Mr. Daniels. Wells and cisterns have often been hiding places over the millennia. And if I remember correctly, the fort's builders installed cisterns in every bastion, did they not?"

"That's right," I said. "Dolores said that each bastion was designed to divert rainwater from the roof down through brick and lead channels into underground cisterns. She showed us the cistern cover in the northwest bastion and told us all about how the cisterns' lead linings poisoned most of the soldiers stationed at the fort. Why didn't we think of it?"

"Because our bastion's half-filled with sand," Kyle said. "We didn't dig deep enough, so we never saw the cistern cover. Outta sight, outta mind."

Mr. Dubois looked pleased by our breakthrough. "Well, sirs, it looks as though you may not have reached a dead end after all. If I could be a young man again, I'd be right there beside you."

Kyle and I both stood. "Thank you, sir," Kyle told him.

"Yes. Thank you very much," I said. "We couldn't have figured it out without your help."

Mr. Dubois waved his hand in dismissal. "The pleasure was all mine. Come again anytime. And boys…"

We paused at the door to look back at him.

"Be sure to keep me apprised of your progress, and if you feel so inclined," he said, lowering his voice, "I would enjoy meeting that lovely lady of yours."

At first I thought he was talking about Linda. It took me a moment to understand that he was referring to the double eagle. I smiled. "Yes sir. We'll try to bring her by."

Chapter 18

The sky was growing dark as Kyle and I walked back down the beach toward the lab. I noticed that both of us had a new spring to our step.

"What do you think about continuing our search now?" I asked Kyle.

"If what Mr. Dubois said is true, that gold's in there waitin' for us to pick it up," he said. "We've gotta get back in that fort. If not tonight, then tomorrow."

"What if the guard's still there?"

"We'll just have to come up with a plan, that's all."

I nodded.

As we approached the marine lab again I was surprised to see lights in the wooden building that served as the wet lab.

"That's weird," I told Kyle. "Let's take a look."

When we reached the lab I peeked through one of the windows, not wanting to interrupt if my dad was giving a lecture or something. Instead I saw that my dad, Linda, and several other students appeared to be packing.

Kyle and I went inside and walked to where my dad was placing some Corning glass flasks into a partitioned cardboard carton.

"What's going on?"

My dad looked up. "Oh, Mike, there you are. Hey, Kyle."

"Hello, sir."

"We thought everyone would be playing volleyball."

My dad straightened up. "Didn't you hear?"

"Hear what?" I asked, thinking maybe the lab had been shut down or something.

"Elsa. She's now up to a Category Four and is heading north. We heard just as we were starting the volleyball game."

"That ain't good news," said Kyle.

"The storm's coming toward Alabama?" I asked.

"They don't know yet. She's still a couple of days out."

"Well, why are you packing up now? Are we leaving?"

"No. Not yet anyway. We're going to stay in session, but if Elsa does head this way we don't want to get caught with our pants down. In fact, I could use some help here."

I looked at Kyle.

"Got nothin' else to do," he said.

With Fort Henry calling us, that wasn't exactly true, but I appreciated his willingness to help out.

Under my dad's supervision Kyle and I started packing up glassware, animal specimens, and fragile equipment from the lab. We'd been working about half an hour when I noticed Rod saunter in. I figured he'd probably been out messing around with Becky, but I didn't let it bother me. After all, who cared about Rod when I was getting to spend more time with Linda? As we all worked Kyle and I joked back and forth with her, and the more I got to know Linda, the more smitten I became. It wasn't only her drop-dead good looks and sweet, honey-smooth voice. She was just *nice*. I vowed that if I ever actually got to be older, I'd find someone like her. Or maybe by then the age difference wouldn't seem so... Well, I could dream, couldn't I?

More students drifted in and we managed to get the whole lab packed up by nine o'clock.

"Whatcha think?" Kyle whispered.

I walked over to where my dad was talking to one of his students. "Excuse me," I interrupted. "Is it okay if Kyle and I take off?"

My dad looked at his watch. "It's already getting kind of late, and I want to get some of our things packed back in the room."

"I can pack my stuff in the morning. It won't take long."

"Alright. Be in by 11:00, okay?"

"Midnight?"

"You stayin' around the lab?"

"Yeah."

My dad relented. "Okay, but don't go taking off down to the village or anything."

"I won't."

I walked back to Kyle. "We're all set."

"Great. Lemme stop by the shop first."

We headed to the workshop between the administration building and the barracks where my dad and I lived. The shop area was surrounded by a chain-link fence with a rolling gate.

"Isn't it locked?" I asked as we approached the gate.

"Naw. Ray usually swings by to lock it up later, but he keeps it open as long as possible so folks like your dad can come in and use it."

Kyle rolled the gate aside and led me to the boat shed, where the lab's two small outboards were parked on trailers. He rummaged around under a workbench. "Here," he said, handing me a crowbar. Then he started searching through drawers in a cabinet labeled "Electronics."

After a moment he held up a wire with connectors on each end. "That's what I'm talkin' about."

From my industrial arts class in junior high school, I recognized the alligator clips. "What are you going to do with those?"

"Watch and learn."

After collecting our flashlights we hurried over to the barbed-wire fence behind the barracks. I was hoping the security guard would have taken off by now, but the car still sat by the front entrance.

"Shoot," I hissed.

"I figured he might still be here."

"What are we going to do?"

"Don't worry, Mike. I got us covered."

Looking warily from side to side, I followed Kyle to the security guard's car.

"Go ahead and let the air outta one of his tires," Kyle whispered. "On second thought, better make that two."

"Why? What're you going to do?"

Kyle walked around to the front of the car. "You'll see." He looked around carefully to make sure the guard wasn't coming, then reached under the hood and popped the latch. "Get goin' on those tires," he told me.

I pulled out my pocketknife and bent down to the rear back tire. I unscrewed the valve cap and paused, glancing over my shoulder. I'd never deliberately damaged somebody's property before, and my pulse felt like a drumbeat in my throat. Then again, I reasoned, I wasn't exactly ruining the tires, just…slowing them down.

I drew out the smallest blade of the knife and pressed the point down on the valve. Immediately air began hissing out of the tire. Kyle was bent over, shining his flashlight down into the engine compartment.

"What are you doing?" I whispered.

"Ah!" he said. "There she is."

I finished deflating the back tire and moved to the front tire. As I unscrewed the second valve cap I could hear a scraping noise from the engine compartment, like wires rubbing together.

"You done?" Kyle asked, straightening up.

"Almost."

He stepped around the front to look at my work. "That'll do it," he said.

I folded up my knife and stood. "Now what?"

He pointed to my left. "Run over to that bastion and

look 'round the corner. Make sure that guard ain't comin' from the other side."

I hurried over and peered around to the fort's north wall but didn't see anyone. I signaled Kyle and watched as he reached back into the car's engine compartment. Suddenly the car horn began blaring. Kyle slammed down the hood of the car and, gripping the crowbar, sprinted toward me.

We ducked around the corner and crouched in the shadows. "How'd you do that?" I asked.

"It was easy," he panted, out of breath. "All you got to do is ground the lead connected to the horn and it sets her off."

From our hiding spot we both looked back at the car as its horn blared away. Every few seconds I checked to make sure the guard wasn't creeping up behind us, but our luck held. After about a minute the guard emerged from the front gate and hurried over to his car. He unlocked the door and climbed in. We could see him pound on the steering wheel, trying to get the horn to stop. Then he got out and walked around the car, scratching his head. That's when he noticed the flat tires. He kicked one of them angrily, and even with the horn blasting away we could hear him cursing. Then he stomped back into the fort.

"What's he doing?" I whispered to Kyle.

"Prob'ly using the fort's telephone," Kyle told me. "Come on, let's go."

"But he's still inside!"

"Yeah, but he ain't worried about us now. He's worried

about his car. By the time he gets help and gets this straightened out, we'll be long gone."

"I hope you're right."

We crawled through the bastion window, but instead of running down through the tunnel we climbed up the circular stairs to the roof. That route let us avoid the central parade grounds but still gave us an easy way to get where we were going. We jogged the rampart, following it clockwise until we came to the closed-off section. We hopped over the chain and then scrambled down to the sand-filled chamber.

"Easy as pecan pie," Kyle said.

"Let's hurry so we can get out of here." My chest felt like a cold fish was flopping around inside.

Kyle lit the lantern.

"Are you sure we should have that on?" I asked.

"Mike, ain't no one goin' to see this from outside. Relax. You're wound up tighter than a yo-yo. We got time. Just show me where we should start diggin'."

In the northeast bastion I had noted that the cistern cover lay directly below the center of the brick arch in the bastion's ceiling. I picked up the shovels and shuffled to the same spot in this chamber.

I handed Kyle a shovel. "Right here."

We both started digging furiously. Fortunately our previous excavations had left the sand in the chamber's center slightly lower than elsewhere. After only ten minutes my shovel struck the flagstone floor. A moment later, Kyle's did too.

"Where's the cistern cover?" Kyle asked, scraping away sand with the blade of the shovel.

Then my shovel hit a smooth metallic surface. I dropped the shovel and brushed away more sand. "Here it is. Help me."

Kyle scraped sand from one side of the cover while I brushed off the other side. Soon we had it clear.

Kyle retrieved the crowbar and wedged it under the heavy metal cover. He grunted, jerking down the crowbar handle.

"You want me to try?"

"I got it." He stuck the crowbar into a new place, like you do when you're prying open a gallon of paint, and again pushed down. When the cover popped up I quickly reached over and grabbed the edge. Together we pulled back the heavy lid. The ancient iron hinge creaked and a swirl of red dust fell away from it.

Kyle shined his flashlight down into the cistern. About two feet below the hole a dark, ominous surface greeted us. "Dang," he said. "It's got water in it! Did our tour guide say how deep these things are?"

"Maybe we can find out." I picked up my shovel and, holding it by the blade, stuck the handle down into the water. When I hit a soft bottom, I pulled the shovel back up. The water mark was about two feet up the handle.

"Well, that's not too bad," I said.

"Yeah, but how're we gonna find out if anything's down there?"

I looked at Kyle and he shook his head.

"I ain't goin' in there, Mike. You know me and water moccasins."

"Well, don't look at me," I objected. "I bet it's full of rats."

"Or maybe the skeletons of soldiers who got thrown down there."

We both stared into the dark water.

"So what're we gonna do?" Kyle finally asked.

I sighed. "I'll go."

Kyle looked at me. "You sure?"

"For a million bucks in gold, yeah, I'm sure." I swung my legs into the cistern hole and sat on the edge.

"You gonna keep your sandals on?"

"Yeah. Who knows what I might step on? Hand me one of the flashlights when I get down there."

With one arm on each side of the hole I lowered myself like I was doing dips on the parallel bars at school. I shivered as my feet touched the water, but not because it was cold—the water wasn't much cooler than it was out in the Gulf. Finally I let go, dropping the final foot with a splash.

My feet sank into a thick layer of mud and the water reached almost to my crotch. I suppressed the impulse to leap back up and out of there and forced myself to breathe deeply.

"You okay, Big Mike?"

My head was now just about even with the level of the hole cover. "Yeah. Give me the flashlight."

I took it and turned it on, then lowered my head down into the darkness. Hunched over, I swung the flashlight wildly around at first, making sure there were no rats or skeletons about to sneak up and give me a heart attack. I expected the chamber to smell like rotting corpses or raw sewage, but only a faint swampy odor reached my nose.

"What's it look like?" Kyle called down.

"It's big," I said, my words bouncing eerily off the walls.

The cistern—as much as I could see of it—looked huge. The chamber where I stood was walled in by brick partitions that apparently held up the flagstone floor above. Each partition, though, had an arched passageway that led into other chambers, and it looked like the cistern probably covered the entire area under the floor of the bastion. Along the walls, I also observed a smooth, reddish surface—some kind of film that must have covered the lead lining they'd installed during construction. I was amazed the lining was still intact or even that the cistern still held water after more than a hundred years.

I continued to shine the light around, double-checking that no rats or snakes were about, but fortunately all I saw were a few spiderwebs. Still bent over, I cautiously moved my feet forward in the mud. My sandal touched something hard.

"Hand me down a shovel," I said.

A wooden handle appeared overhead and I took it. I reached down with the blade and scooped up the thing in front of me.

"Ya got anythin'?"

I pulled out a thick, coiled spring and handed it up to Kyle.

"Looks like part of a car suspension," he said.

I kept feeling around and found more junk along with several dozen bricks, which I dropped back into the water. As I moved away from the overhead opening, though, the junk disappeared and I was left with just the layer of muck on the cistern bottom. Using the shovel handle and my feet, I explored the entire chamber for any little bumps in the mud layer, but found none. Then, nervously counting my teeth with my tongue, I waded to one of the arches that led to adjoining chambers.

The arch was low and only cleared the water by about a foot. To get through it I was going to have to lower myself down into the water to my neck.

Don't think about it, I told myself. Holding the flashlight over my head, I quickly dunked myself down and through into the next chamber.

"You okay?" Kyle's voice sounded far away.

"Yeah," I called back, though I'd never been so unsure of anything in my life.

Dripping now, I started shuffling and poking along methodically as I'd done in the first chamber. Suddenly something cold and slimy brushed my leg.

I hollered, dropping the flashlight and shovel into the water. Darkness smothered me. Panicked, I lunged back toward the arch but couldn't see where I was going. My head smacked into the brick partition and, ears ringing, I fell gasping back into the water. Another long, slimy thing swept across my chest and I let out a second yell.

"Mike!" Kyle shouted and I saw a dim light through the

archway. As fast as I could, I scrambled toward it.

"What happened?" Kyle said as I pulled myself back up through the cistern hole.

"Something's down there!" I panted, shaking badly.

"What? What's down there?"

"I-I don't know!"

Kyle bent down into the hole and shined his flashlight into the water while I sat shivering, trying to get a hold of myself. After a moment, I heard Kyle's muffled voice say, "I'll be danged! Eels!"

"What?"

His head popped back up. "There's eels in there, Mike. A swarm of 'em!"

"No way."

"I swear."

I took the flashlight and looked for myself. Sure enough, a long slender body slithered underneath the light. A moment later I saw smaller fish—minnows.

"How the hell did *they* get in there?"

"Don't know," said Kyle. "There's gotta be some kind of passage to the sea."

"Geez!" I gasped. "I thought I was a goner."

Kyle chuckled and a moment later we were both laughing hard, breathless laughs.

"So what do you wanna do?" Kyle asked. "Should we beat it outta here?"

The thought strongly appealed to me, but I shook my head. "No. We've come this far. Let me explore the rest."

Kyle whistled. "You're braver than me."

I knew that wasn't true, but it made me feel bolder to hear it.

I lowered myself back down into the water, and Kyle handed me his flashlight. I ducked back into the second chamber and, shuffling my feet, found both the shovel and the ruined first flashlight, which I returned to Kyle. Then, forcing myself to take long, regular breaths, I continued my search.

Altogether there were about a dozen chambers, but I explored each one carefully. At any moment I expected to stumble across a wooden chest or a pile of coins, especially in the chambers farthest from the cistern opening.

I found nothing.

By the time I returned to the opening and Kyle helped me back up onto the sand, I was again shaking—from cold this time.

"It's n-not in there," I said.

"You sure?" he asked.

"I'm sure. I c-covered every square inch of that place. The gold isn't there."

Kyle lit a cigarette and offered it to me. I shook my head.

He sighed. "Well, I guess we could go check the other cisterns, see if that historian guy overlooked somethin'."

"No. If it isn't in this one, it isn't in any of them. Let's get out of here."

Kyle stood up and stubbed out his cigarette. "You don't have to tell me twice."

Chapter 19

By the time I woke up late the next morning my dad had already left for breakfast. I was glad. It gave me a chance to lie in bed feeling sorry for myself.

As soon as Kyle had brought up the idea that the gold was hidden in the cistern, I'd been rock-solid certain he was right. To come up empty-handed...well, it pretty much crushed our fantasy of striking it rich. Sure, we could keep looking through the fort, but after the previous night, my enthusiasm had abandoned me. I tried to console myself with the fact that at least we had one double eagle, but compared to a whole chest full of them, a single coin didn't seem like much.

After twenty minutes of replaying the previous night's events, I sighed and swung myself into a sitting position. I pulled on some shorts and headed over to the dining hall. Fortunately Louella and Evelyn were happy to fix me up with a late breakfast, and by the time I'd finished eating, my mood had rebounded a bit.

Back at our apartment I pondered what I needed to

pack. It didn't look to be an overwhelming job. Everything I had would fit into the bags I'd brought with me from California. My dad had some textbooks in addition to his clothes, but nothing I couldn't handle. While I worked I turned on the radio to catch any updates on the hurricane. Elsa, the announcer said, was churnin' and burnin' four hundred miles out into the Gulf and was expected to make landfall in thirty-six to forty-eight hours. The good news for us was that she appeared to be headed somewhere between Galveston, Texas, and Lake Charles, Louisiana, hundreds of miles to the west of us. Still, I'd heard about hurricanes changing course without any warning. I agreed with my dad that it would be smart to be prepared in case she suddenly turned her attention our way.

I finished packing in less than an hour, basically shoving everything we owned into our bags and a couple of cardboard boxes I'd scrounged from the back of the mess hall. I did take special care with my coin collection, however—and of course I had to figure out what to do with the double eagle. I didn't want to put it with the rest of my coin collection because that would be too obvious if a thief—or a captain—happened to be looking for it. After reviewing my options, I settled on sticking it under the lining of my left running shoe. Even if someone did come looking for it, I didn't think they'd bother to tear apart my stinky shoes. Also, gold was pretty inert. A little sweat wouldn't hurt the coin any.

Of course, the double eagle raised a couple of bigger issues that I'd put off thinking about. The first went back to what the captain had said. Did Kyle and I really have any right to keep the double eagle since we'd found it in a historic site? On the one hand, if we hadn't found the coin, I doubt anyone would have, and that should count for something. On the other hand, we did find it on public property, so the State of Alabama could also make a case for it. I'd talked it over with Kyle and he'd said I was crazy for even thinking about turning it in, but it still gnawed at me.

The second issue was that if we did decide to keep it, who was going to get it, me or Kyle? Technically I'd found the double eagle by sticking my toe in the sand, but I never would have found it if Kyle hadn't taken me to the fort. I figured the coin was as much his as it was mine. But the problem with coins is you can't just split one of them in half. How would we decide?

I realized I didn't have an answer for either of these dilemmas, so I decided to put off thinking about them until we knew for sure when we'd be leaving the island. After securing the coin I stuffed the shoe into my workout bag and walked through the apartment one last time. Satisfied I'd done all I could, I went looking for Kyle.

I found him at the lab offices, helping his stepfather Ray nail sheets of plywood over the windows.

"Hey," I called as I approached.

"Hey," Kyle answered.

Ray nodded in my direction and mumbled a greeting. Even though I'd been on the island more than a month, I'd rarely talked to the man. He was at least ten years older than my father—probably in his late forties or early fifties—and he always seemed to hang back from the other people at the lab. Still, after hearing the stories Kyle told me about him, I figured he had to be a pretty good guy.

"Is everyone ready for the storm?" I asked.

Ray took one last whack at a nail and reached for another one. "Ain't nobody ever ready for a storm the size of this one."

"I was just listening to the radio and they're thinking it's not going to come this far east."

"Let's hope not," he said. "But we kin use all the hands we kin get."

The hint wasn't exactly subtle, but I'd intended to help out anyway. Kyle and I took over boarding up windows while Ray went off to attend to other matters.

"How's it going?" I asked after Ray had left.

Kyle shrugged and muttered, "It's goin'."

I picked up a sheet of plywood and carried it to the next window. "What's wrong?" I asked, assuming that Kyle was still disappointed about not finding the gold.

He reached down and pulled a half-dozen nails from a blue and yellow box on the ground. "I'm just hopin' this hurricane gives us a wide berth."

I was surprised Kyle would be worried about a storm. I held the plywood in place over the window. "Don't you think it'd be kind of fun to see what it's like?"

Kyle hammered in a nail. "You don't know what you're talkin' about, Mike. Hurricanes ain't fun. If you're in the middle of one, they're scarier than hell."

"Oh yeah. I know," I said, stung by the rebuke.

Kyle pounded in another nail and I let go of the sheet of wood. "Besides," he said, his voice softening, "it ain't so much the storm. I just don't want to leave this place."

"Yeah," I said, a twinge of sadness settling into my chest. "I know what you mean. I was hoping we'd have more time to find that treasure."

Even as I said it, though, I realized that the gold had very little to do with what I was feeling. The sadness came from the thought of losing a friend.

Kyle pounded in another nail and then glanced around to make sure no one was listening. "Mike," he continued, his face as solemn as I'd ever seen it. "I ain't never told nobody this, but Ray…he's got some problems."

Of course, Kyle had already told me his family moved around a lot and that Ray didn't always get along with his bosses, but this sounded like something more serious.

Kyle's voice dropped even lower. "Ray fought in Korea."

"I didn't know that."

"Yeah. And the thing is, it messed him up somehow. I mean, he's usually fine, but he slips into these black funks. I guess you'd call 'em depressions."

I paused, then asked, "What's that like?"

"Sometimes he gets mean. Other times it's like he just crawls deep inside himself and ain't no one can get him out again."

I wasn't exactly sure what to say. "Has he seen a doctor or anything?"

"Lots of 'em. They give him medicine, but Ray don't

like takin' it. Says it makes him feel like somebody else. He throws the stuff away and won't go back again."

"Oh."

Kyle clutched the hammer with both hands and stared out toward the Gulf. "So anyway, we get to a new place and he works for a while and everything's goin' fine. Then all of sudden he falls back into one of his funks and blows up at the boss or just don't go to work at all. Next thing you know we gotta pick up and start all over again."

"Geez. He's seems fine to me."

"I know. That's just it. Lately he's been better than I ever seen him. I was hopin' we could settle down on the island for a while. Here he can work on his own, make his own schedule. He ain't never stayed on a job this long."

"Oh," I said. "I see."

"So it ain't just the storm I'm worried about, Mike. It's Ray and my mom and Annie. If Elsa takes this place out, well, I don't know…"

I nodded.

His eyes swung back toward me. "Well, hell, I figured with your parents split up and all, you might understand."

I thought back to the worst day of my life—the day five years earlier when my dad took me out into the field next to our apartment house in California and told me he was leaving. It was like someone had reached into my chest and pulled out my heart in one swift tug. I'd never told anyone, but nothing in my life had ever been the same after that.

I looked back at Kyle. "Yeah," I said. "I understand."

Chapter 20

K yle and I spent the rest of the day hauling plywood and nailing it up over windows. We also used a hand truck to load several boxes of important records into the lab director's Travelall so he could drive them back to his house on the mainland. After dinner we decided to visit Fort Henry one last time.

We approached the barbed-wire fence but stopped when we could see the parking lot. Sure enough, the security guard's car had returned—with four fully inflated tires and probably a functioning horn too. The guard was sitting in a lawn chair next to the car, all business, wearing dark sunglasses and tapping a nightstick in his hands.

Kyle snorted. "Guess he weren't too happy about last night."

I laughed. "Yeah, I guess not. I still can't believe we did that."

"No big deal. It gave him somethin' to do at least."

"You still think the captain of the *Reef Wrecker* has something to do with this new security guy?"

"I ain't got the slightest doubt."

"Me either. You want to try and get back in so we can look some more?"

"Do you?"

I sighed. "I don't know. I thought for sure the gold was in that cistern. Since it wasn't...I mean, we could look forever and never find anything more. Even if the coins are in there, that place has so many nooks and crannies and hiding places, we'd have to tear it all down to have a chance of recovering them."

"I think you're right, Big Mike." He slapped his hand on my shoulder and added, "But it was fun lookin'."

"Yeah. It was."

Even though I'd spent the last few weeks desperately hoping we'd find the gold, I had to admit I felt a bit relieved the search had ended. I sensed that Kyle felt the same way.

We started back in silence. When we'd almost reached the barracks Kyle asked, "Wanna go over to the gym and shoot some baskets?"

"Sure. Let's go."

* * *

"Hey," my dad called when I got back to our apartment later that evening.

I walked through the bathroom to his room. "Hey. What're you doing?"

He pushed back his chair. "Just trying to get organized. Thanks for packing up."

"No sweat."

"I heard you and Kyle worked all day around the lab."

I shrugged. "We didn't really have anything else to do. Any news on Elsa?"

My dad lit a cigarette and exhaled. "Yeah. She's three hundred miles off now, heading for New Orleans at thirteen miles per hour. If she hits there it's going to be a monumental disaster."

"How come?"

He took another puff. "The city's below sea level, surrounded by levees. If one breaks, the whole ocean will pour in."

"But in a way that's good for us, right? We'll be too far away for any real damage, won't we?"

"We'll get some big waves and some fifty- or sixty-mile-per-hour winds, but we should be okay."

"Will they evacuate the island?"

"Not unless Elsa changes course dramatically."

While my dad finished his work for the evening I entered the latest grades for his class into his grade book. Around nine-thirty he pulled out the cribbage board. While we played I once more debated if I should tell him about the double eagle. Once again I decided not to. There would be time later, after we left the island, I reasoned. Even more important, my cribbage cards were red-hot. I was having too much fun whipping my dad to risk spoiling the mood.

* * *

My dad shook me awake early the next morning. At first I thought he was exacting his revenge for my cribbage victories, but when he snapped at me to hurry it up I knew something serious was going on.

I rolled over and yawned. "What's going on?"

"Elsa's changed course and picked up speed. She's heading right toward the Alabama coast."

"What?" I sat up, fully awake. "You're kidding."

My dad's jaw tightened. "No joke. They're expecting her to hit about ten o'clock tonight. All the teachers and students are going over to the lab to get things battened down."

"What do you want me to do?"

"You're welcome to pitch in, but there'll be plenty of people to handle the lab. Why don't you go find Kyle and see if his family needs anything?"

"Okay."

My dad paused at the door with his hand on the knob. "The most important thing," he said, "is to be ready to go by four o'clock sharp. The National Guard wants everyone off the island by six o'clock, so make sure you're back here by three at the latest."

I threw on my clothes, opting for my running shoes instead of my usual sandals since I figured the day might involve a lot of running around. As I put on the left shoe I could feel the lump made by the double eagle, and I debated whether or not to take it out. *No,* I decided. *This way I'll at least know where it is.*

As I crossed the parking lot toward the mess hall my body buzzed with the excitement of the impending storm. I looked up at the bands of gray clouds overhead. Little gusts of wind hit my face and I could hear the waves crashing from the beach, but the day didn't look especially ominous. It was hard to imagine that just a few hours from now all hell might break loose.

Inside the mess hall I found Kyle eating breakfast with Annie.

"So, looks like we're in the bull's-eye," I said, sitting down with my plate of eggs, hash browns, and toast.

"Looks like it," Kyle said.

"You ever been in a hurricane before?"

"I've been close enough to know when to be scared."

"You guys leaving?"

Kyle nodded. "Early afternoon. You?"

"Same thing. You need help getting ready?"

He shook his head. "Naw, we're all set."

"What about Ray?"

"I think we did most everything yesterday."

As I washed down a bite of eggs with a gulp of milk, a thought popped into my head.

"Kyle, maybe we should go over and check on Mr. Dubois. He said his kids are in Atlanta. Maybe he needs a hand packing up."

Kyle drained his cup of coffee. "Good idea. Annie, tell Mom where I went."

"Do it yourself," she shot back.

Kyle winked at me. "You ever wanna go fishin' again?" he asked her.

"Oh, all right," Annie relented.

"You're a peach," he said, tweaking her cheek.

"Stop!" she squealed, but she couldn't hold back a smile.

* * *

Five- to six-foot breakers crashed onto the shore as we walked toward Mr. Dubois' house. Even though the tide was supposed to be out, the waves rolled up high on the beach.

"These are the biggest waves I've ever seen in the Gulf."

"Just wait," Kyle said. "I'll bet they're twice that big by this afternoon."

"Too bad we don't surf."

Kyle looked at me, eyes twinkling. "I thought everyone from California surfed."

"And I thought everyone from Alabama made moonshine whiskey."

Kyle laughed, but I heard a tightness in his voice. Even though the storm was hours away, it already seemed to press down on the island.

Mr. Dubois wasn't sitting in his usual spot on the porch, so we climbed the back steps and knocked. We heard footsteps and a moment later the door opened.

"Well, boys, glad to see you back again. Come on in."

I expected conversation to turn quickly toward the storm, but I was wrong.

"So," Mr. Dubois asked the moment we stepped inside, "any new developments in the great gold mystery? Please tell me that you've found it."

"No sir," Kyle told him. "But we got the largest collection of post–Civil War bottle caps this side of Pensacola."

Mr. Dubois let out a hearty laugh. "Very good, boys. I see our other treasure hunters are still at it."

Kyle and I looked out into the Gulf and watched the *Reef Wrecker* bob up and down in the swell.

"Yeah, we saw that," I said. "Do you think they'll try to ride out the hurricane?"

Mr. Dubois chewed on his pipe stem. "I doubt the Coast Guard will let them, but you can bet they will resist leaving until the very last minute, especially if they have discovered something."

"Ya think they have?" Kyle asked.

Mr. Dubois shrugged. "Who can say? The *Skink* could have been carrying other treasures besides the gold."

"Yeah," Kyle said. "Never thought of that."

"What about you?" I asked Mr. Dubois. "You're going to leave, aren't you? We came over to see if you need any help with packing or boarding up your windows."

The old man seemed amused. "Oh, I don't think I'll be going anywhere. I'll close up the shutters, of course, but this house has weathered many a hurricane. I believe she'll stand up to one more."

Kyle looked at me and frowned.

"But Mr. Dubois," I pressed. "Do you think that's such a good idea? My father said the storm surge could wash over the entire island. They're evacuating everyone from the lab. Me and Kyle could get you packed up and ready to go in a few minutes."

"That's right," added Kyle. "We could at least get your valuables loaded."

Again the man smiled. "I'm grateful for your offer, boys. I really am. But you reach a certain age and you're…uh, how should I put it? You're content to let nature take her course."

An uncomfortable feeling fluttered through my chest. "Are you sure? I mean, I've never been through a hurricane, but Elsa sounds like a bad one."

Mr. Dubois laid a gentle hand on my shoulder. "I appreciate your concern, boys. I will be all right. Now please indulge me and turn your energies back to the things that matter. Your families. And," he added with a wink, "the gold."

"Oh," I said, slipping off my left running shoe.

Mr. Dubois looked at me quizzically.

Kyle said, "You're not going to dump sand on Mr. Dubois' floor, are ya?"

"Very funny." I reached under the lining of the shoe and removed the plastic envelope containing the double eagle. I slipped the coin out of the plastic and handed it to Mr. Dubois.

"You said you wanted to see her."

Mr. Dubois must have had some familiarity with coins, because he naturally took the coin by its edges and tilted it back and forth in the gray light. He didn't say anything for a few moments, and I noticed moisture in his eyes.

"That, gentlemen," he said, his voice raspy, "is one of the most beautiful things I've had a chance to see in this life."

"She is pretty, ain't she?" Kyle said.

Mr. Dubois looked at the coin for another minute, handling it with reverence. He handed it back to me. "I do thank you for the gift of bringing it by."

Of course I didn't tell him that it had pretty much been an accident, being in my shoe and all.

"Allow me to return the favor," he said.

Mr. Dubois hobbled out of the room and returned a moment later holding out his grandmother's diary.

"Did you want to show us something in it?" I asked, confused.

Mr. Dubois smiled. "No, I want you two to keep it for me." He pressed the book into my hand.

I immediately tried to hand it back to him. "I can't," I said. "We can't." My heart pounded with the thought of safeguarding such a treasure.

"No sir," Kyle agreed. "That book ought to be in a museum."

Mr. Dubois just smiled and pushed the diary back to me. "No, I think you are the perfect keepers of it."

"W-why?" I stammered, still alarmed at the thought.

"Well, for one thing, the younger generation of my family is not that interested in the history of us old-timers. For another, as I said, my grandmother was just about your age when she wrote it. If her thoughts and experiences will mean anything to anyone, they might mean something to you."

Kyle frowned. "You sure 'bout this?"

"I'm sure, Mr. Daniels."

"What if we just borrow it for a while?"

Mr. Dubois chuckled. "If that's what it takes to seal the deal, so be it."

We reluctantly said goodbye to the old man and headed back down to the beach.

"Geez," I said, looking at the waves. They already seemed a lot bigger than they had an hour ago. "He can't stay here."

Kyle scratched at his cheek. "No, he can't. Not without committin' suicide."

"It almost sounded like that's what he wanted to do. And what's this all about?" I asked, holding up his grand-mother's diary.

"Ya got me. When he handed us that book, it was like a ghost flew right through me."

"You think he's crazy?"

"I don't know, but we'd better tell somebody he ain't fixin' to leave."

* * *

As soon as we got back to the lab we went to the office and told Mrs. Stevenson, the lab administrator, about Mr. Dubois. While we hovered nearby she called the county sheriff, but got a busy signal.

"They must have their hands full today," she said. "But don't worry, I'll keep trying 'til I get through."

Not knowing what else to do, we headed back to the mess hall. Because of the hurricane, Louella and Evelyn were rushing to put everything away in the kitchen. Instead of a regular lunch, they'd placed out salads and cold cuts so people could make their own sandwiches. Kyle and I made ourselves triple-decker ham, salami, cheese, and lettuce sandwiches and heaped our plates with potato salad. While we ate, people hurried in and out, grabbing a quick bite and returning to their tasks.

As we left the mess hall a gust of wind tore the door handle from my hand, and a cloud of dust and sand flew into our eyes. The sky had grown darker, and thick ropes of angry clouds swirled from one horizon to the other. A fully loaded Ford Pinto with two students in front drove past us toward the lab exit. I felt a few drops of rain land on my skin, and a feeling of urgency began building in my chest.

"Well," I said, "I'd better go back and see if my dad needs any help."

"Yeah, I might need to help my folks too," Kyle said. "See ya later."

Kyle took a step, then stopped abruptly and turned back to me.

It occurred to us both at the same moment: we might *not* see each other later.

"Oh geez," I muttered awkwardly. "When do you think you're going to leave?"

"Me, my mom, and Annie are prob'ly going to head out pretty quick. Ray's bringin' his truck just as soon as everyone from the lab is ready to go. What about you?"

"My dad said four o'clock, but maybe sooner if we get ready."

We stood staring at each other, an uncomfortable silence hanging between us.

Finally Kyle stuck out his hand. "Well, Mike. If this hurricane scores a direct hit there prob'ly won't be much to come back to."

I wasn't quite ready to say goodbye. I again removed my left running shoe and pulled up the lining.

"Mike," Kyle said. "What're you doin'?"

I handed him the double eagle. "I want you to have this. You grew up in the South. It'll mean more to you."

Kyle took the gold coin and held it up in the dim light of the dark sky. He tilted it back and forth like Mr. Dubois had done, enjoying the full details of the face. He flipped it over. "Mm-hmm," he said. "She's a beauty, all right." Then in one quick motion he grabbed my right wrist, opened my palm, and slapped the coin into it.

"What are *you* doing?"

"He-ell, Mike. You found it. 'Sides, I wouldn't have the faintest idea what to do with it."

"Just keep it. Or sell it."

"You kiddin' me? If that thing's real, it's gotta be worth, what, a hundred grand?"

I looked down at the coin's Confederate reverse. "More, probably. And you can bet it's even going to get more valuable."

"That's what I mean," he said. "You'll know better how and where to sell it when the time comes. Afterwards, you can write me a big fat check for my share."

I started to argue with him, but he shook his head. Without thinking I slipped the coin into my right front pocket.

"Well," he said, again extending his hand. "'Til next time."

I met his grip. "Yeah. It was great meeting you—I mean, hanging out with you."

"Yeah," he said, letting go. "Maybe we can meet up here next summer—if this storm doesn't blow the lab away."

"I hope so," I said.

"Say goodbye to your dad."

"You too. To your folks and Annie, I mean."

"Alright, then."

"Alright."

With his left hand he made a peace sign and, with a last grin, turned away.

Chapter 21

I found my dad in the wet lab building. I expected others to be there too, but he sat alone on a stool sliding some last notebooks into a cardboard box.

"Where is everybody?" I asked.

"Students are all gone. The farther away from here, the better. News reports said Elsa's holding at Category Four and has a good shot at Five before she makes landfall."

"Sounds bad."

"It's going to be bad, all right."

"So are you done here?"

"Just about, but they've called a last-minute staff meeting over at the office."

"How long will that take?"

"Don't know. Hopefully not more than an hour. Can you put these in the car?" He handed me the cardboard box.

"Sure."

"I want you ready to split as soon as this meeting is over. Where'll you be?"

"I guess I'll hang out in the mess hall."

"Good enough."

It had grown so dark that the lab's outdoor lights had automatically clicked on, and it looked like nine or ten at night, not the middle of the day. The wind had really picked up too, buffeting me as I walked. I wrapped my arms around the cardboard box as if it were an anchor and squinted to protect my eyes from the billowing sand. I was also beginning to understand the term "pelting rain" and wondered where exactly I'd packed my raincoat.

As I reached our VW Squareback, something small and hard cracked the top of my head.

"Ow!"

I glanced down to see a piece of gravel bounce on the ground. Turning my eyes skyward, I saw that the wind was blowing pebbles off the barracks' tar and gravel roof. One of them pinged off the hood of the VW. *Good thing those aren't bricks up there*, I thought, remembering the one that had almost brained me in the fort.

And that's when the lightbulb finally went on in my head.

"Holy crap!" I exclaimed.

I threw my dad's notebooks into the VW and sprinted toward Kyle's house. "Please let him still be there," I muttered as I ran.

As I approached his place I saw the family's '63 Buick still parked in the oyster shell drive. I pounded on their front door.

"Kyle!"

The door flew open. "What the he-ell?"

"Kyle," I panted, out of breath. "I know...I know where the gold is."

His eyes widened. "What? You sure?"

"Yes. No, I'm not positive...but...well, shoot. Come on!"

Kyle glanced through the door into his living room and then looked back at me. "Mike, if this is some wild goose chase—"

"No, it ain't—I mean, it isn't. It just came to me, but we've got to hurry."

He studied me for another second, then went back inside. I could hear him arguing with his mom. In a few seconds he reappeared. "You'd better be right about this, Yankee."

We ran as fast as we could across the lab property to the barbed-wire fence. Wind and rain blasted our faces as we ran, but I hardly felt them. At the fence we paused, sopping wet, to examine the parking lot.

"Not a soul in sight," I said. "They've probably closed the fort because of the storm."

We ducked through the fence and raced to the northwest bastion. I boosted Kyle inside the fort and he pulled me up after him.

"Now what?" he asked.

"We need a ladder or scaffold or something."

"I remember seein' a toolshed when we took that tour."

"Let's go."

We ran through the tunnel out to the parade grounds.

Kyle led me to a wooden door at the back of the old officers' quarters. The door was unlocked and we ducked inside. Against the wall I spotted an eight-foot stepladder.

"That'll do it." I lowered the ladder and we each took one end, me in front.

"I can't believe you talked me into this," Kyle yelled as we hurried toward the steps that led to the ramparts. "Where we goin'?"

"Back to the same place," I shouted, straining to make my voice heard over the shrieking wind.

"We don't have time to dig through that sand again!"

"We won't have to!"

When we reached the top of the ramparts we were almost blasted off our feet. The winds had to be blowing at least fifty miles per hour—high enough to turn the metal ladder into a crude sail. Kyle and I struggled to keep it pointed directly into the wind so we wouldn't be knocked down—or worse, swept off the top of the fort. The wind had whipped up the ocean too. Huge waves, twelve to fifteen feet high, rolled in toward shore like armies on the march. We staggered forward, and I could feel the fort shake as each breaker smashed directly into the southeast bastion—the one closest to the sea and, it turns out, our destination.

"Look!" Kyle shouted.

I glanced back and saw two long, swirling gray serpents rising out of the water, reaching all the way up into the clouds. They looked like tornadoes but were over the ocean. I didn't know such a thing even existed.

"Waterspouts!" Kyle yelled.

The strange monsters were still way offshore and looked to be heading away from us, but that didn't blunt the first cold blade of fear slicing through me.

We finally reached the southeast bastion and worked the ladder awkwardly down the slippery stairs. Once we were inside the sand-filled chamber the only thing that separated us from the ocean's fury was the ancient five-foot-thick brick wall of the fort.

"Mike, you sure 'bout this? This place looks like it might come crashin' down any second."

As Kyle spoke, a wave thundered against the fort with such force that it knocked chunks of brick and mortar from the ceiling above us. If I hadn't been so sure where the gold was, I would have been three steps ahead of Kyle, running for my life. But I just *knew*, and that certainty drove me forward.

"Let's set up the ladder here," I told Kyle, walking to the spot where I'd found the first double eagle.

"We already dug here."

"I know," I said. "But this time we've got to climb."

The worry on Kyle's face turned to concentration, then revelation. "Of course!" he shouted. "Man, it was starin' at us the whole time! It ain't *under* us. It's *above* us!"

"Yeah," I said. "I can't believe we didn't figure it out sooner."

"You think they bricked it into the ceiling?"

"Maybe," I said. "But it's more likely they buried it next to the cannon up on top of the bastion. I figure the chest probably rotted away and the coins just made their way down to the brick right above us."

"Yeah, maybe in those channels they made to catch rainwater," Kyle said.

"Yeah."

We set up the ladder and, after testing it, I climbed. If the chamber had been empty, the ladder wouldn't have reached the ceiling, but with so much sand in the place, I got right up to it. Straining my eyes, I tried to examine the bricks and mortar above me.

"How's it look?" Kyle called.

Even though a little light came into the chamber from the stairwell and through the smaller hole at the far end of the ceiling, the storm clouds made it impossible for me to make out any details.

"It's too dark. I can't see," I told Kyle.

"Hold on a sec." Kyle let go of the ladder and got the Coleman lantern that we'd accidentally left in the chamber on our last visit. He fired it up and handed it to me.

The bright light allowed me to get a good look at the ceiling. The brick and mortar directly above me looked pretty solid, the bricks ranging in color from red and orange to almost black. Many of them were cracked, but mortar and friction still seemed to be holding them together. As I moved the light slowly out in different directions, though, I saw places where chunks of mortar and entire bricks had fallen out onto the sand below.

I climbed back down and set the lantern on the sand.

"See anythin'?" Kyle asked.

Another monster wave slammed into the fort, startling both of us. More debris rained down from the ceiling. "Let's move the ladder over."

We scooted it over a few feet, made sure it was solid, and then I ascended once again with my back toward the stairs that led down into the chamber. Now I looked up at a more ragged section of the ceiling where much of the mortar had crumbled and fallen into the sand below.

Holding the lantern in my left hand, I reached up and gently touched the rough edges above me.

"Easy, Mike," Kyle said, again shouting to make his voice heard above the roar of the wind outside. "That stuff looks like it could all collapse if you breathed on it wrong."

As if to punctuate his warning, another giant wave pounded the fort. I clutched the ladder, feeling it wobble, and then resumed my examination of the ceiling.

I held the lantern up close, moving it back and forth and trying to peer into every crack and crevice. I was just about to climb back down to move the ladder again when my eyes caught a dull metallic glint from deep within one of the holes. My breath caught. Had I just imagined it?

I swung the lantern slowly back over the spot. There it was again.

My impulse was to tear away the brick, but I knew that might send the whole ceiling crashing down. Instead I carefully probed the crevice with my fingers. I dug them in as far as I could, but they were too thick to reach the glinting metal.

"Shoot!"

"What's wrong?" Kyle yelled.

"You have anything long and flat, like a screwdriver or a pocketknife? I packed my knife away this morning."

Kyle felt his front pockets. "Naw. Nothin'." He reached into his back pocket. "Hold on." He pulled out a black plastic comb and handed it up to me.

"Perfect," I said.

"Whatcha got?"

"Just a minute."

Still holding the lantern in my left hand, I worked the comb into the bricks. It was just long and slender enough to reach what I hoped was another coin. I pressed the comb's teeth delicately against the edge of the metal and began drawing it slowly toward me.

"Ya find anything?" Kyle shouted.

"Yeah," a man's deep voice echoed behind us. "Ya find anything?"

Chapter 22

I froze. Slowly I looked over my shoulder. Two dark figures stood silhouetted at the base of the stairs. Without even thinking I gave a last tug on the comb. Something yellow flashed by the corner of my eye, but I didn't try to follow its path. Instead I held the lantern out. "Who is it?" I asked, guessing that the intruders were from the *Reef Wrecker*.

The two figures moved slowly toward us. As they came into the light of the lantern I could see that one of them was small and slender while the other stood tall, with hair that looked like a poofed-out sea sponge.

"Well, if it ain't Rod and Becky," Kyle said. "You come to join the other rats runnin' around the fort?"

"You might want to clamp down on that mouth of yours," Becky said. Rod pointed a pistol straight at us.

Kyle held up his hands. "Hey, whatever you say. You're the boss."

I saw Rod's teeth gleam eerily in the glow of the

lantern. "Now you're getting the idea. Get down from there," he ordered me, motioning with the gun.

I stepped down a couple of rungs and handed the lantern to Kyle. He bent over and placed it deliberately on the sand next to the ladder.

"Step over here," Rod said. "Slowly now, slowly. That's it." When we got within ten feet of them he told us to stop. "Now," he said, still pointing the gun at us, "I understand that you two might just have outsmarted a million-dollar salvage operation."

"We ain't got the faintest idea what you're talkin' about," Kyle said.

Another wave thunderclapped against the fort, and I saw both Rod and Becky flinch. Rod's eyes grew more serious. "Oh yeah, you do. Becky told me all about her nice conversation with the captain. We've been watching you two come in and out of this fort for the last week—long enough to know you aren't just digging for seashells."

"So where's the gold?" Becky demanded.

"What gold?" Kyle said.

"Why, you little—" Rod stepped toward Kyle, his gun raised to strike him.

"Wait!" I shouted.

Rod shifted his glare from Kyle to me. A bright flash of lightning filled the cavern, followed a second later by a sky-splitting boom. "Well?" he demanded.

I looked over at Kyle. "We might as well tell them."

"Mike, don't tell them nothin'."

"It's no use now. They've got the gun. Let's just let them have the gold and get out of here."

"Good boy," Becky said. "Now you're talking sense."

"It's up there," I said, pointing to the brick ceiling above the ladder. "We were just trying to get it out when you walked in."

Becky's eyes rose to the chamber ceiling, then fixed back on me. "Oh, come on. You're tellin' us you've been in this fort for weeks and you only just found the gold today?"

"I swear. We dug through all this sand without finding a thing. It just occurred to me this morning that the coins were hidden in the ceiling. Why else would we come here now, in the middle of a hurricane?"

"Oh," Becky sneered, "and you just happened to know to look here in this very spot?"

"No ma'am," Kyle said. "We looked all over this crazy fort, but this was the only place that made sense."

"Look for yourselves," I said. "It's right up there."

Becky and Rod glanced at each other, the greed sparking like electricity between them. "Empty your pockets," Becky said. "I want to make sure you didn't already take any."

My gut leaped into my throat and I had a horrifying realization. *The original double eagle was still in my pocket!*

"They're empty," I croaked, feeling weak.

"Don't mess around with me. Let's see those pockets."

I reached into my left front pocket and slowly pulled the liner inside out.

"Now the other one," she said.

I pulled out the liner of the right pocket, palming the double eagle.

Becky didn't fall for it. "Now hold out both hands."

I had no choice. I did as she said.

Kyle saw what I was holding and let out a moan. "Mike—"

"That's what I'm talkin' 'bout!" Becky shrieked. "Rod, get that coin."

Rod obeyed, leaving no doubt who was truly in charge of this operation. Reluctantly I handed over the double eagle.

I expected Becky to tell Kyle to empty his pockets too, but she didn't—probably because he hadn't been the one up on the ladder.

Instead she demanded, "Now, where's the rest?"

"We told you," I said, pointing to the chamber ceiling. "They're up there, behind the bricks."

"Here," Rod said, handing Becky the gun. "You watch these punks while I check it out."

"Stand over there and don't move," Becky ordered us. We stepped back while Rod picked up the lantern. He tested the ladder and climbed to the top.

By this time Kyle and I had moved about twenty feet toward the stairwell. "That's far enough!" Becky yelled at us. "Stay there or I'll shoot you, I swear," she snarled, gripping the gun with both hands.

I noticed the pistol shaking slightly in her hands and I looked at Kyle. He stared hard back at me, as if trying to convey a message.

Rod reached the top of the ladder and felt around the brick with his fingers. "I don't see anything."

Another wave pummeled the fort and the wind outside howled.

"It's hard to see," I told him. "But I know I saw it. You have to get behind the brick. I was just about to pull one out when you got here."

Using his free hand, Rod pulled out a pocketknife and opened the blade with his teeth. He began chipping away at the crumbling mortar. While we all stared, he grasped a brick and slowly worked it loose. It came away in his hand, almost causing him to lose his balance. I watched in amazement as half a dozen golden flashes streaked by the lantern and fell to the sand below.

Becky squealed and rushed to the base of the ladder. She picked up a coin triumphantly and shouted. "We got it! We got it!"

Kyle nudged me and nodded toward the stairs. I took a step back. Becky wheeled around, straining to hold the gun steady. "Don't even think about it, boys!" Without turning, she asked Rod, "Do you see any more?"

He held the lantern up to the spot. "Yeah, but I've got to enlarge this opening."

"Do it!" Becky ordered.

Twin flashes of lightning illuminated the chamber, followed by cannon-fire thunder.

Rod reached up and tugged on another brick. He couldn't pull it free so he set the lantern on top of the ladder. He hacked at the mortar with his knife, then, using both hands, he yanked hard on the loose brick.

Suddenly a huge section of ceiling came crashing down. A cascade of brick, mortar, dirt, and gold coins knocked Rod off the ladder and buried him. The lantern went out, plunging the chamber into gloom.

"The gold!" Becky yelled, dropping the gun and scrambling toward the rubble.

"Let's go!" Kyle hissed.

Without looking back, we raced up the stairs.

When we emerged onto the top of the bastion, the wind nearly knocked us off our feet. Just as we tried to recover our balance a giant wave hit the fort, sending a fountain of water up and over the wall. Drenched, I looked out toward the dark horizon and could hardly tell where the sky ended and the sea began. Huge, rolling swells barreled into shore. They had already engulfed the dry moat below us, and I could see that water would soon completely encircle the fort.

"Come on!" Kyle screamed. "We gotta run!"

I was about to follow when something out in the waves caught my attention. "Look!"

Kyle followed my gaze. A mile offshore the *Reef Wrecker* was desperately trying to thread the gap into Mobile Bay. She was already listing badly, and as we watched, a huge breaker crashed over her stern. We saw one man, arms flailing, swept over the port side and several others scurry toward the bow, trying to escape the ocean's wrath.

Kyle seized my arm. "They're done for. We gotta git!"

With the wind at our backs we raced along the fort ramparts and back down the wide brick ramp to the parade grounds. Without stopping, we hurried through the tunnel and out the hole in the northwest bastion. Fortunately the seawater had not yet made it to this side of the fort, so our way to the lab was clear. Less fortunately, we now had to run straight into the wind and rain.

We hunched over and sprinted back toward the lab. The slashing raindrops stung my face. I could barely keep my eyes open, but we finally reached the barbed-wire fence and struggled through. Then we ran as hard as we could toward the mess hall. My dad spotted us as we reached the parking lot.

"Dammit, you two! I've been looking everywhere for you!"

"We're sorry!" I shouted. "We—"

"Never mind! Kyle, your mom and sister already left. Your dad's waiting in the truck at your house. Can you get there okay?"

"Yeah, but Dad!" I said. "Rod and Becky! They're trapped in the fort!" It had occurred to me not to tell anyone—as I'm sure it had to Kyle—but in the end, gold thieves or not, it just wasn't right to leave them.

My dad stared at us. "*What?*"

"Rod…Becky," I panted. "Some bricks fell on them in the southeast bastion of the fort."

"What the hell were you doing at the fort?" he demanded. "Are they all right?"

"I don't think so!"

My dad shook his head and took a deep breath, trying to decide what to do. "Okay, I'll run to the office and see if I can get the sheriff. Mike, you get in the car. We're leaving as soon as I make the call, understand?"

My dad raced toward the lab office and Kyle and I stood staring at each other through the driving rain. It was our second goodbye that day, and given the circumstances, there was only one thing to say.

"Did you get it?" I asked.

His blue eyes gleamed. "Better," he said, rain streaming down his face. "I got *them*."

He reached into a back pocket and pulled his hand out. Two shiny gold coins sat in his palm.

"*Two* of them fell?"

A grin cracked his face as he handed me a coin. "Now we each got us a souvenir."

I glanced briefly at the coin and stuffed it into my pocket. Then I reached out my hand and Kyle seized it.

We stood there, hands clasped for a moment. Then Kyle released his grip.

"See ya later, Big Mike."

"Yeah. Later."

With that, he turned and disappeared into the rain.

Chapter 23

My dad hoofed it back to our VW and leaped in, wetter than a porpoise. As he turned the ignition I noticed that only two other cars besides ours remained in the parking lot.

"Are the police coming?" I asked. I felt as guilty as I'd ever felt in my life—not about Rod and Becky, I admit...they'd made their own choices—but about putting my dad through so much worry.

"Phone line was dead," my dad said, throwing the car into reverse. "We'll have to try to find someone on the way out."

"Did you tell Dr. Halsted?"

My dad paused at the lab gate, looked both ways, and then gunned the car out onto the road. "Bob took off an hour ago," he said. "He thought Becky had left this morning in one of the student vans. He was planning to meet up with her in Mobile."

That, I thought with a shudder, *is a rendezvous that is*

never going to happen. Suddenly I felt very bad for the professor.

"What were you two doing at the fort anyway?" my dad demanded.

On the way back to the lab, Kyle and I had agreed to try to tell the truth as much as possible. "We thought we'd found the gold," I said, watching the water sheet across the roadway ahead of us.

A huge pine branch slammed down onto our hood and we both jumped. It slid a few inches, then blew off the other side.

My dad glanced over at me. "You *what?*"

"The Confederate gold the *Reef Wrecker* was looking for," I explained. "Kyle and I thought we'd found it."

Anger flushed my dad's face. "You mean while I was racing all over, worried that you'd drowned or been swept away, you two were on a *treasure hunt?*"

I nodded, the guilt swelling inside of me.

"Is that why Rod and Becky were there too?"

"No. Yes. I mean, I think they'd been watching us and wanted to steal whatever we found. They followed us over there and that's when the brick collapsed on top of them."

My dad's jaw clenched and unclenched as he seemed to chew over what I'd told him. The roar of the wind filled the car and the VW's windshield wipers swiped furiously at the rain. Fallen branches were strewn all along the roadside. We heard a loud crack and then a swooshing sound. An entire pine tree crashed onto the pavement behind us.

My dad glanced in the rearview mirror, but didn't slow down.

After driving in silence for a few moments, he turned to me. "Did you find it?" he asked.

"What?"

"The gold. Did you find it?"

For a split second my brain was paralyzed. *Should I tell him the whole story? What would he say about the coins Kyle and I had kept?*

Then I made my decision. "No," I said, not because I didn't trust my dad or didn't want him to know. It was more like this was something Kyle and I had done on our own. For now, at least, I wanted to keep it that way.

My dad sighed again and shook his head. His jaw relaxed. "Son, promise me you will *never* do anything like that again."

"Okay."

"Okay what?" he said, for emphasis.

"I promise."

* * *

By the time we reached the village the wind had begun to rip power lines from their poles. The island was more protected here on the lee side, but I could see that the water had already risen high enough to completely cover the salt marsh. The wind bent the palm trees over at right angles, and a five-foot chop was tossing around boats like toys in the marina. One thirty-foot sailboat had already torn loose from its berth and slammed into a pleasure cruiser fifty feet away. It wouldn't be long before others started breaking loose.

I glanced at Mr. D'Angelo's store as we drove by and saw the windows and door covered with plywood. An image of Mr. Dubois alone in his house flashed into my head and I wondered if the authorities had evacuated him. But before I had time to think any more about it we approached the bridge entrance.

The Alabama National Guard had set up a checkpoint here, evidently to turn back any people crazy enough to try to reach the island from the mainland. My dad braked our VW to a stop and opened the window.

A soldier in heavy rain gear came over to us. "You need to get out of here."

"Understood," my dad answered, "but we've got a couple of people possibly trapped down at Fort Henry."

The soldier glanced around and walked over to another uniformed man. They conferred briefly and the second man approached us.

"You've got some people missing?"

"Yes. My son saw a man and a woman get trapped by falling brick in the fort."

The man bent down and peered through the window at me. "That right, son?"

"Yes. They're inside the southeast bastion. The ceiling collapsed on them."

"Are they hurt?"

"I think so. My friend and I ran for help."

The man straightened up and removed a portable radio from his belt. He spoke into it, relaying what I'd told him. "We'll get someone down there," he said to us, "but y'all need to leave right now. We have reports of tornadoes in the area and with the high water, we don't know if this bridge'll hold."

"Thank you, officer," my dad said.

We crept slowly out onto the bridge. The structure was an old one, constructed in the 1930s, and it ran more than three miles straight across the sound that separated Shipwreck Island from the mainland. It had been built flat as a rail line and stood on angled concrete pylons fifteen feet above the normal water level. Now, however, I saw that the ocean churned and swelled only about five or six feet below the tops of the pylons. Worse, I could feel the bridge actually shift and move under the brunt of wind and water. No other traffic drove ahead or behind us, and I got the definite feeling that we shouldn't be there either.

"This is scary," I shouted to my dad above the roar of the wind.

"You said it," he agreed, hunched over and trying to see through the torrents of water cascading over the windshield.

"I guess most people already got out."

"I hope so. Right before you showed up the National Hurricane Center issued a bulletin that Shipwreck Island and Mobile are directly in Elsa's path and she's moving even faster than predicted. That's why I got so worried about you. I'll bet we've only got an hour or so before the eye passes right over here."

Still, as we neared the steel drawbridge in the center of the span, I was starting to feel like everything was going to be okay. Then I looked back.

"Dad, look!"

What we saw looked like the planet's Messenger of Death. Rising like an apocalyptic genie into the sky, the swirling black tornado reached from the horizon all the way up into the hurricane's corded cloud layers. It spit out lightning bolts as if Zeus himself were riding it. Worst of all, the twister bore directly down onto the east end of Shipwreck Island.

My dad swore quietly, but even his oath couldn't begin to capture the tornado's immensity and fury. We slowed and watched.

"It looks like it's heading right toward the marine lab," my dad said.

"And the fort."

The black monster churned forward at remarkable speed. Even from a distance I saw it suck up trees and pieces of buildings as if they were dust. Then a car rose into the sky.

"Let's get out of here," my dad said, slamming his foot on the accelerator.

* * *

We drove north from Shipwreck Island with the hurricane growing more fierce by the minute. The road followed the west side of Mobile Bay most of the way, offering us little protection from Elsa. Gusts of wind slammed the side of our car, threatening to send us sliding off the two-lane highway. Power lines slithered across the ground like black snakes. We stopped twice to help people move trees off the road. By now drainage ditches overflowed and in one little town floodwater came up to the middle of our hubcaps.

For the first fifteen miles or so we saw only a few other cars besides police cruisers and National Guard vehicles. Entering Mobile, however, we hit a snarl of traffic created by hundreds—probably thousands—of others trying to flee Elsa's wrath. The Guard had closed the Bankhead Tunnel and the eastbound interstate to Pensacola, so we were forced to drive west, toward New Orleans.

While we crawled forward in bumper-to-bumper traffic, the eye of the storm passed over Mobile. Fortunately we were on Elsa's less-powerful side. We learned later that the storm had weakened to a Category Two around the time she reached us. Still, high winds continued to send debris flying. I saw a huge gust tip over a mobile home next to the interstate and an oak tree crash down through someone's roof. Billboards and signs were shredded like tissue paper and, in one low-lying part of town, water flooded dozens of cars almost to their roofs and reached up onto people's front porches.

We drove at a snail's pace until almost midnight and

ended up spending the night in a hurricane shelter—a high school auditorium—outside of Biloxi, Mississippi. By that time the winds had subsided to thirty- and forty-mile-per-hour bursts. Relief workers gave us a hot meal and blankets, then pointed us toward two cots over near the bleachers. The faces around us looked haggard with fatigue and worry, but most people stayed awake listening to a portable radio spit out nonstop accounts of the storm's toll of destruction. It wasn't until the following morning, however, that Elsa's true magnitude became apparent.

* * *

Elsa was the worst storm to hit southern Alabama in half a century. Four years earlier the legendary Camille had mainly targeted Mississippi, leaving Alabama relatively unscathed. As reports began coming in over the next few days, we saw how lucky we had been to get out of Elsa's way.

Elsa had plowed a path directly through Shipwreck Island. Television and newspapers showed pictures of almost total destruction of the island. Eighty percent of the trees had been blown over. Out near the west end the hurricane had actually cut a new channel all the way through the island. The marina was a total loss, with only four of the hundred-plus boats left afloat. More than half of the bridge to the mainland had disintegrated. From the news reports it sounded like every single building had either been destroyed or received massive damage.

The loss of life was equally horrendous. Forty-six people were reported dead and dozens more were missing. We heard nothing about Rod, Becky, or Mr. Dubois, but the Coast Guard reported that the *Reef Wrecker* had sunk with no survivors. Search and Rescue crews were still picking up bodies all around Mobile Bay.

Once my dad and I got back to his house in Pensacola I sat glued to the television, looking for some news of Fort Henry. I saw nothing until the second evening. We were eating TV dinners in front of the six o'clock news when the local CBS station aired a report on Shipwreck Island. The reporter first explained that despite the almost total destruction of buildings on the rest of the island, SCUM-Lab had survived remarkably intact. The tornado we'd seen had turned the old recreation hall, officers' houses, and other wooden buildings into piles of plywood and two-by-fours, but the barracks, administration building, mess hall, and other concrete structures had come through the storm with minimal damage.

"Wow," my dad said, looking visibly relieved. "Looks like the Air Force's nuclear planning paid off."

"Yeah." I shoved a forkful of peas and potatoes into my mouth, but my eyes remained fixed on the television as the camera swung around to Fort Henry.

"Unfortunately," the reporter continued, "the fort that survived Civil War battles and half a dozen previous hurricanes could not stand up to Elsa."

As the reporter blathered on, the camera panned across the main entrance to the fort.

"That doesn't look so bad," I said to my dad.

"No, it doesn't."

Then the cameraman walked around to the fort's southern wall.

I dropped my fork. "Geez, look at that!"

The nearest part of the south-facing wall looked like a hundred cannons had all fired directly into it at point-blank range. The once stubborn-looking defenses had been reduced to piles of bricks barely half the wall's former height. Looking farther down the wall, I felt the hairs on my neck stand to attention.

"The southeast bastion is totally gone!"

"Shhh!" My dad turned up the volume. "Listen."

"Twenty-foot waves combined with a deadly tornado completely swept this section of the fort out into the Gulf," the reporter chirped. "In fact, you can see where the ocean scoured a new channel right into the center of what used to be Fort Henry's parade grounds. Authorities still have no word on the two people reported trapped in the fort when the tornado and hurricane struck."

My dad and I looked at each other. "Rod and Becky," I said.

My dad nodded and turned down the volume. "I was waiting to tell you this, Mike," he said. "I spoke to Professor Halsted earlier today."

I had picked up my fork again, but I held it empty over the dinner tray. "What did he say?"

"Apparently the National Guard did send a team down to the fort, but just as they got there, the tornado came ashore. The Guard vehicle was lucky to escape, and immediately afterward all of them were ordered off the island."

"So no one knows if Rod and Becky made it out?"

My dad pushed his tray away and wiped his mouth with a paper towel. "Not with certainty, but it doesn't look good. The police would like to talk to you about what happened. You feeling up to that?"

"I...guess so."

"They want to talk to Kyle too, but no one has been able to track down his family."

* * *

All that evening and the next morning I worried about what I'd tell the police. *Should I tell them everything that really happened? Should I tell them that we'd actually found the gold? What if they found Kyle and he gave them a different story?*

The next afternoon a Pensacola police officer named Dennis came out to our house. He was a young guy, about six-foot-one with a pleasant but businesslike demeanor. My dad sat with me as I answered the man's questions.

I had feared that the police would really grill me like lawyers did on *Perry Mason* and other television shows, trying to trip me up and find every flaw in my story. This interview went nothing like that. The officer first asked me why I was in the fort. Until that moment I hadn't decided what to say, but I decided to stick to the story Kyle and I had agreed on. I told him that Kyle and I thought we'd found the gold, but instead we had come up empty-handed.

To my surprise, the officer didn't seem all that interested in the gold, probably putting it down as the fantasy of a couple of teenage boys. He went on to ask me why Rod and Becky had shown up, and then asked about their personal relationship. When I told him about seeing Rod and Becky kissing and holding hands together, he just nodded his head knowingly.

"It's not the first time a love tryst has gone bad," he said.

He asked a few more questions, scribbling notes on a small flip pad. Then he closed it and stood up.

"Thank you for your time," he told me, shaking my hand.

We walked him out to the front porch. As his cruiser pulled away my dad turned to me and said, "You okay, son?"

I took a deep breath and nodded.

Chapter 24

I didn't see or hear from Kyle Daniels again. After I got back to California I wrote him a letter, but then I realized I didn't have his address in Birmingham. When I talked to my dad during one of our weekly Sunday night phone conversations, I asked him to get it for me. The next week he told me that most of the records from SCUM-Lab had been destroyed by the hurricane.

Undaunted, I called information for Birmingham and excitedly scribbled down the phone number and address they gave me. I called, but got a recording that the line had been disconnected. I took a chance anyway and sent my letter to that address. It boomeranged back a few weeks later with a red stamp reading "No forwarding address. Return to sender." I thought about trying his aunt in Mobile, but I had no idea what her name was or even where she lived. Reluctantly I gave up my search. Every couple of nights, though, I dug out the double eagle and admired it. I hoped that somehow Kyle and I would both end up on Shipwreck Island again the next summer.

Against all odds SCUM-Lab did reopen for classes, and my dad was again invited to teach the summer course in invertebrate zoology. I was thrilled until, a few weeks before I flew to Florida, my dad gave me the bad news that Kyle's family would not be there.

"Did they just not want to hire his dad?" I asked on the phone, remembering what Kyle had told me about Ray's past.

"I don't think it was that," my father replied. "I don't think Ray even sent in an application. No one has any idea where they are. I'm sorry, son."

* * *

When my dad and I finally did get to Alabama I was stunned by what awaited me. They hadn't even begun to rebuild the bridge to the island, and we had to ride a little ferry across the Intracoastal Waterway. What I found on the other side was a complete disaster. Even a year after the storm, gutted homes and piles of rubble covered Ship-wreck Island. About half of the paved roadways had been washed out. Repairs had barely begun on the houses that still stood, and hulks of wrecked ships littered the jetties and beaches around the marina. Instead of the sounds of waves and peaceful breezes through the pines, the roar of chain saws, bulldozers, and jackhammers filled the air. Even I could see that restoring the island was going to take years.

Things were moving a bit faster out at SCUM-Lab.

Bulldozers had scraped away the remains of buildings that had been destroyed, and repairs had been completed on the main administration building and dining hall. The roof of the barracks, however, had leaked badly during the hurricane, and the inside of the building had to be totally gutted and replaced. While repairs were going on, trailers were brought in to house the students and faculty. The trailer my dad and I shared was clean and, unlike the barracks, had a fully functioning air-conditioner. But I missed the funky old barracks with its musty smell and the rec room down below.

I missed the people too. Linda had graduated, much to my disappointment. Dr. Halsted had understandably decided not to return. My second afternoon there I walked down the beach, hoping to find that Mr. Dubois and his house had somehow survived Elsa. It was wishful thinking. All along the beach the storm surge had flattened the sand dunes, and even from a distance I saw an empty lot where the old gray house should have been. I asked around about Mr. Dubois, and most people thought he'd gotten off the island. Recalling my last conversation with him, however, I had my doubts. I even wondered if he really did have children in Atlanta, like he'd told us.

One thing that hadn't changed—at least not very much—was Mr. D'Angelo's market. When my dad and I arrived by ferry that first day I smiled seeing the store's new roof and fresh coat of paint. A new sign advertised Mr. D's famous tamales, and over the next few weeks I made a point of jogging or hitching a ride down there for lunch as often as possible. The first time I came in, he bellowed, "Hey, Mike! How was California? I'm glad our lil' old storm didn't scare you away, because boy have I got some coins for you!"

But looking through the coins he saved for me was about the only thing I really enjoyed that summer. The new students were friendly and I even went on a lot of my father's field trips with his class, but my heart wasn't in it. The days crawled by like a slug moving across a dusty gravel road.

I missed Kyle. I missed our adventures together.

Our last day there I walked over to the fort—or at least to the chain-link fence that now surrounded its ruins—and stared at the gaping hole that used to be the southeast wall and bastion. Even seeing it for myself I found it hard to believe that a storm, any storm, could so thoroughly obliterate such a massive structure.

It had.

Nothing remained of the place where Kyle and I had discovered the double eagles. The bricks, the gold, and everything else—even Becky and Rod, as far as I knew—had been swept out into the Gulf of Mexico or Mobile Bay. A part of me had been swept away with it. Not that that was all bad. Hearing Kyle's wise voice in my head, I realized that it was just how things went. "He-ell," Kyle would have told me. "Somethin' new will take its place."

I nodded and laughed to myself. Then I waved goodbye to the fort and left Shipwreck Island for the very last time.

November 7, 2009

From the *Conglomerated New Services,*
November 7, 2009:

Confederate Gold Piece Packs Double Surprise
One of two previously unknown
double eagles fetches record price

New York City—When the final gavel struck last night
at the Feldman Auction House in downtown Manhat-
tan, a previously unknown Confederate gold piece
had sold for a record-shattering price of 18.9 million
dollars. The coin, an 1861 twenty-dollar gold piece or
"double eagle," sent shock waves through the coin-
collecting community when it was unveiled by an
anonymous collector earlier this year. Coin collectors, or numismatists, received a second jolt when a
second, almost identical, double eagle was produced
the following week by a different collector.

Until their appearance, no one in or out of the coin-
collecting community had any proof that the Confederate States of America had minted gold coins with
their own designs. However, a panel of historians,
chemists, metallrgists, and numismatists hastily
assembled to verify the coins' authenticity. After two
months of tests and research, both coins were certi-
fied as genuine. Harvard Civil War historian Geoffrey
Dawson called the coins the most important Confeder-
acy-related discovery in a decade. "Since the war
ended," Professor Dawson explained, "people have

speculated that the Confederates had hidden reserves of gold bullion. This find not only lends support to those claims, but indicates that the South intended to proceed with its own bullion-based currency."

The double eagles quickly became the subjects of closed-door negotiations between the coins' owners, the Federal Government, and the State of Alabama, where the coins are rumored to have been discovered. At a press conference held last month, Feldman's announced that the first coin would be put up for auction. In a separate statement issued the same day, the Smithsonian Institution announced that the second coin had been donated to the museum's permanent collection. It is not clear if or how the two announcements were related.

What is clear is that last night's auction smashed all previous records for a price paid for a single coin. Bidding opened at $4 million and continued for more than forty-five minutes, with more than thirty parties involved from twelve different countries. The winning bid surpassed the previous record for a coin by more than ten million dollars.

Don't you wish you had one?

the end

Author's note

Although *Double Eagle* is a work of fiction, like all good yarns it has its roots in real places, events, and people. I would like to point out to interested readers some aspects of the book that are based on facts and others that exist purely in my imagination.

With regard to the Civil War, the general details about the defense of Mobile Bay are true, but I have changed the names of people and locations and fiddled with some timelines for the story's sake. The mouth of Mobile Bay, for instance, was defended by two forts, Fort Gaines and Fort Morgan. Both were short on heavy artillery. However, it was rumored that the commander of the entire bay's defenses was getting kickbacks from blockade-runners smuggling goods in and out of the bay. That likely explains why Fort Morgan, which overlooks the smugglers' main access channel, had more cannons and was better defended than Fort Gaines.

Mobile Bay was also the last Confederate port on the Gulf of Mexico to fall into Union hands, not just because it was so well defended but also because of inept orders by Union generals, which delayed an attack on the bay and city of Mobile. As indicated in the novel, the Union's Admiral Farragut wanted to attack Mobile as early as 1862, but was instead ordered on other missions that largely proved to be a waste of time. This delayed the capture of Mobile until 1864.

As far as the Confederate double eagle is concerned, I am sad to say that no such coin is known to exist. It is true, however, that Confederate treasurers did mint four silver half-dollar test patterns with a Confederate reverse design. It is also true that when the New Orleans Mint was first handed over to the State of Louisiana (and later to the Confederate States of America), a half-million dollars in bullion was still sitting in the mint in the form of foreign gold and silver coins. The state of New Orleans and the Confederacy melted down these foreign coins to mint fresh U.S. gold and silver coins.

All told, the state of New Orleans minted 9,750 double eagles. Once the mint was turned over to the Confederacy an additional 2,991 gold double eagles were minted. To make these double eagles, the Confederacy used the old Union dies. To the naked eye the coins are indistinguishable from those minted under Union control. Some experts believe that those minted under the Confederacy can be identified by careful examination of cracks and other details on the coins, but I don't know about that. What I do know is that if the Confederacy *had* used their own designs to mint double eagles, those coins would be among the most valuable and sought-after in the coin-collecting world today.

So what happened to the double eagles minted under Confederate control? Speculation and some evidence indicate that a portion of this gold may have ended up at local New Orleans banks and that much of it was passed on to the Confederacy. It appears that Confederate officers may also have buried a large number of the double eagles outside the city, and that these were never recovered. We may never know the exact fate of these coins, but the search for this missing treasure continues to this day.

Regarding hurricanes, there was no Hurricane Elsa. Since the 1960s, however, coastal Alabama has been hammered by at least five major hurricanes. Dauphin Island, which I used as inspiration for Shipwreck Island, took a direct hit from Hurricane Frederic in 1979. The storm demolished the drawbridge to the mainland, hundreds of homes, and a fair portion of the Dauphin Island Sea Lab. In 2005, Hurricane Katrina took another swipe at the island, destroying more than one-third of the homes on the island's west end and washing an oil rig up on shore. Amazingly, Fort Gaines—"Fort Henry" in the story—received almost no damage from either of these storms, a testament to the remarkable workmanship that went into the fort. The fort does, however, sit perilously close to the ocean and is therefore vulnerable to future erosion and hurricanes.

For those who would like to learn more about life in Mobile and the defense of Mobile Bay during the Civil War, I recommend the following books:

Confederate Mobile by Arthur W. Bergeron Jr., University Press of Mississippi, 1991.
Blockade Runners of the Confederacy by Hamilton Cochran, University of Alabama Press, 2005.
A Blockaded Family by Parthenia Antoinette Hague, University of Alabama Press, 1991.

For a terrific summary and history of the New Orleans Mint, I recommend the following article: "The New Orleans Mint" by Greg Lambousy, published in the March issue of the *Numismatist*. A link to the article can be found at *http://lsm.crt.state.la.us/NO_Mint_Numismatist.pdf*.

Of course, anyone who can should visit Fort Gaines, located at the eastern tip of Dauphin Island. While you're there, check out the wonderful estuarium built by the Dauphin Island Sea Lab. Whether you find gold or not, it's a trip you'll remember.

Thank you!

Researching *Double Eagle* has been one of the most pleasurable experiences of my career, thanks largely to the incredible hospitality and efforts of the people who offered their knowledge, creativity, and just hard labor.

First and foremost I would like to thank the folks at Dauphin Island Sea Lab. From its humble beginnings as a converted Air Force base, this facility has grown into one of the finest educational and research institutions on the Gulf Coast. Everyone at the lab extended my family and me every consideration. I would especially like to thank the former director George Crozier for inviting me to stay at the lab, Pamela Pierce for setting up housing, John Dindo for taking me behind the scenes throughout the facility, Ashley Foster for patiently answering my myriad questions, and Jenny Cook and the entire educational staff for teaching me about local animals and plants. At the lab I would also like to thank Melissa, Shane, and Sam for keeping me "well connected"; the maintenance staff for keeping our baby stroller rolling; housekeeping for keeping us warm; the dining hall for offering up the island's best meals; and the people at the Estuarium for allowing us to roam around unchecked.

I'd also like to thank the enthusiastic staff at Fort Gaines, especially historian Joseph Everett, who not only gave me a terrific tour of the fort but came up with several important ideas for the plot. Melinda Oalmann and Ursula Prince at the fort extended me every courtesy. I am also grateful to Greg Lambousy, the director of collections at the Louisiana State Museum, for cheerfully providing fascinating information about the history and activities at the New Orleans Mint during the Civil War years.

My additional thanks go to the helpful people of the Mobile Public Library and the Museum of Mobile, who eagerly pointed me toward a number of important reference materials on blockade-running, the defense of Mobile, and other aspects of local history. The quote on page 81 is from *A Guide Book of United States Coin: 27th Revised Edition* by R. S. Yeoman.

Once again I am indebted to my father, Sneed B. Collard Jr., for his recollections of Dauphin Island, his unparalleled knowledge of the Gulf of Mexico, and his comments on the manuscript.

As always, my writers' group—Hanneke, Jeanette, Dorothy, Peggy, Wendy, and Bruce—helped to set me on the right course in the book's early stages. *Muchas gracias!*

A special thank you to the Lighthouse Bakery for cooking us the most delicious Thanksgiving dinner ever and providing all of the pastries and mochas we could ask for.

Double Eagle nor any of my other novels could have flourished without the skillful editing and patience of my editor Vicky Holifield, and the enthusiastic dedication of the entire crew at Peachtree Publishers. Thank you once again!

Finally I would like to thank my wife Amy, my son Braden, and my daughter Tessa for goin' South with me to research and enjoy one of America's real hidden treasures—southern Alabama. I couldn't have done it without y'all.

The author at Dauphin Island Sea Lab

SNEED B. COLLARD III is a biologist, speaker, world traveler, and the author of more than fifty books for young people. His middle-reader novel, DOG SENSE, won a 2005 Henry Bergh Children's Book Award, and his YA novel, FLASH POINT, received the 2007 Green Earth Book Award and appeared on the 2007 Bank Street Best Children's Books of the Year list.

Collard was recently honored with the distinguished Lud Browman Award for his achievements in scientific writing. In 2006, he won the prestigious Washington Post/ Children's Book Guild Nonfiction Award for his body of work.

To learn more about Sneed and his books, explore his website at *www.sneedbcollardiii.com.*